Penguin Book 2487
Idiots First

Bernard Malamud was born on 26 April 1914 in
Brooklyn, New York. He took his B.A. at the
City College, N.Y. and his M.A. at Columbia.
After various odd jobs, he began to teach in 1939.
At the present time, he teaches English at Benn-
ington College where he lives with his wife and
two children.

In short stories such as these, Bernard Malamud
acknowledges the influence of Chekhov, James
Joyce and Hemingway. He has also written *The
Natural* (1952), *The Assistant* (1957), which won
the Rosenthal Award, *The Magic Barrel* (1958),
which won the National Book Award U.S.A. for
1959, and *A New Life* (1961). He is working on
his fourth novel, which should be finished in 1966.

Bernard Malamud

Idiots First

Penguin Books
in association with
Eyre & Spottiswoode

Penguin Books Ltd, Harmondsworth, Middlesex, England
Penguin Books Pty Ltd, Ringwood, Victoria, Australia

First published in the U.S.A. 1963
Published in Great Britain by Eyre & Spottiswoode 1964
Published in Penguin Books 1966
Copyright © Bernard Malamud, 1950, 1959, 1961, 1962, 1963

Made and printed in Great Britain by C. Nicholls & Co. Ltd
Set in Linotype Granjon

The stories in this book, all slightly revised, appeared in the following
magazines: *Commentary*, *Esquire*, *Harper's Bazaar*, *Partisan Review*,
Playboy, *Saturday Evening Post*, *The Reporter* and *World Review (London)*.
An excerpt from the scene from *Suppose A Wedding* appeared in the
New Statesman.

PLEASE NOTE: Professionals and amateurs are hereby warned that the
scene from *Suppose A Wedding* is fully protected under the copyright laws
of the United States and all foreign countries, and is subject to royalty.
Permission for performances and readings, on any medium, must be secured
from the author's agent, Diarmuid Russell, 551 Fifth Avenue, New York 17,
New York.

Women and children first OLD SAYING

For Ida and Gino

Contents

Idiots First

The thick ticking on the tin clock stopped. Mendel, dozing in the dark, awoke in fright. The pain returned as he listened. He drew on his cold embittered clothing, and wasted minutes sitting at the edge of the bed.

'Isaac,' he ultimately sighed.

In the kitchen, Isaac, his astonished mouth open, held six peanuts in his palm. He placed each on the table. 'One ... two ... nine.'

He gathered each peanut and appeared in the doorway. Mendel, in loose hat and long overcoat, still sat on the bed. Isaac watched with small eyes and ears, thick hair greying the sides of his head.

'Schlaf,' he nasally said.

'No,' muttered Mendel. As if stifling he rose. 'Come, Isaac.'

He wound his old watch though the sight of the stopped clock nauseated him.

Isaac wanted to hold it to his ear.

'No, it's late.' Mendel put the watch carefully away. In the drawer he found the little paper bag of crumpled ones and fives and slipped it into his overcoat pocket. He helped Isaac on with his coat.

Isaac looked at one dark window, then at the other. Mendel stared at both blank windows.

They went slowly down the darkly lit stairs, Mendel first, Isaac watching the moving shadows on the wall. To one long shadow he offered a peanut.

'Hungrig.'

9

In the vestibule the old man gazed through the thin glass. The November night was cold and bleak. Opening the door he cautiously thrust his head out. Though he saw nothing he quickly shut the door.

'Ginzburg, that he came to see me yesterday,' he whispered in Isaac's ear.

Isaac sucked air.

'You know who I mean?'

Isaac combed his chin with his fingers.

'That's the one, with the black whiskers. Don't talk to him or go with him if he asks you.'

Isaac moaned.

'Young people he don't bother so much,' Mendel said in afterthought.

It was suppertime and the street was empty but the store windows dimly lit their way to the corner. They crossed the deserted street and went on. Isaac, with a happy cry, pointed to the three golden balls. Mendel smiled but was exhausted when they got to the pawnshop.

The pawnbroker, a red-bearded man with black horn-rimmed glasses, was eating a whitefish at the rear of the store. He craned his head, saw them, and settled back to sip his tea.

In five minutes he came forward, patting his shapeless lips with a large white handkerchief.

Mendel, breathing heavily, handed him the worn gold watch. The pawnbroker, raising his glasses, screwed in his eyepiece. He turned the watch over once. 'Eight dollars.'

The dying man wet his cracked lips. 'I must have thirty-five.'

'So go to Rothschild.'

'Cost me myself sixty.'

'In 1905.' The pawnbroker handed back the watch. It

had stopped ticking. Mendel wound it slowly. It ticked hollowly.

'Isaac must go to my uncle that he lives in California.'

'It's a free country,' said the pawnbroker.

Isaac, watching a banjo, snickered.

'What's the matter with him?' the pawnbroker asked.

'So let be eight dollars,' muttered Mendel, 'but where will I get the rest till tonight?'

'How much for my hat and coat?' he asked.

'No sale.' The pawnbroker went behind the cage and wrote out a ticket. He locked the watch in a small drawer but Mendel still heard it ticking.

In the street he slipped the eight dollars into the paper bag, then searched in his pockets for a scrap of writing. Finding it, he strained to read the address by the light of the street lamp.

As they trudged to the subway, Mendel pointed to the sprinkled sky.

'Isaac, look how many stars are tonight.'

'Eggs,' said Isaac.

'First we will go to Mr Fishbein, after we will eat.'

They got off the train in upper Manhattan and had to walk several blocks before they located Fishbein's house.

'A regular palace,' Mendel murmured, looking forward to a moment's warmth.

Isaac stared uneasily at the heavy door of the house.

Mendel rang. The servant, a man with long sideburns, came to the door and said Mr and Mrs Fishbein were dining and could see no one.

'He should eat in peace but we will wait till he finishes.'

'Come back tomorrow morning. Tomorrow morning Mr Fishbein will talk to you. He don't do business or charity at this time of the night.'

'Charity I am not interested –'

'Come back tomorrow.'

'Tell him it's life or death –'

'Whose life or death?'

'So if not his, then mine.'

'Don't be such a big smart aleck.'

'Look me in my face,' said Mendel, 'and tell me if I got time till tomorrow morning?'

The servant stared at him, then at Isaac, and reluctantly let them in.

The foyer was a vast high-ceilinged room with many oil paintings on the walls, voluminous silken draperies, a thick flowered rug at foot, and a marble staircase.

Mr Fishbein, a paunchy bald-headed man with hairy nostrils and small patent leather feet, ran lightly down the stairs, a large napkin tucked under a tuxedo coat button. He stopped on the fifth step from the bottom and examined his visitors.

'Who comes on Friday night to a man that he has guests, to spoil him his supper?'

'Excuse me that I bother you, Mr Fishbein,' Mendel said. 'If I didn't come now I couldn't come tomorrow.'

'Without more preliminaries, please state your business. I'm a hungry man.'

'Hungrig,' wailed Isaac.

Fishbein adjusted his pince-nez. 'What's the matter with him?'

'This is my son Isaac. He is like this all his life.'

Isaac mewled.

'I am sending him to California.'

'Mr Fishbein don't contribute to personal pleasure trips.'

'I am a sick man and he must go tonight on the train to my Uncle Leo.'

'I never give to unorganized charity,' Fishbein said, 'but

if you are hungry I will invite you downstairs in my kitchen. We having tonight chicken with stuffed derma.'

'All I ask is thirty-five dollars for the train ticket to my uncle in California. I have already the rest.'

'Who is your uncle ? How old a man ?'

'Eighty-one years, a long life to him.'

Fishbein burst into laughter. 'Eighty-one years and you are sending him this half-wit.'

Mendel, flailing both arms, cried, 'Please, without names.'

Fishbein politely conceded.

'Where is open the door there we go in the house,' the sick man said. 'If you will kindly give me thirty-five dollars, God will bless you. What is thirty-five dollars to Mr Fishbein ? Nothing. To me, for my boy, is everything.'

Fishbein drew himself up to his tallest height.

'Private contributions I don't make – only to institutions. This is my fixed policy.'

Mendel sank to his creaking knees on the rug.

'Please, Mr Fishbein, if not thirty-five, give maybe twenty.'

'Levinson !' Fishbein angrily called.

The servant with the long sideburns appeared at the top of the stairs.

'Show this party where is the door – unless he wishes to partake food before leaving the premises.'

'For what I got chicken won't cure it,' Mendel said.

'This way if you please,' said Levinson, descending.

Isaac assisted his father up.

'Take him to an institution,' Fishbein advised over the marble balustrade. He ran quickly up the stairs and they were at once outside, buffeted by winds.

The walk to the subway was tedious. The wind blew mournfully. Mendel, breathless, glanced furtively at shadows. Isaac, clutching his peanuts in his frozen fist, clung to his father's side. They entered a small park to rest for a minute on a stone bench under a leafless two-branched tree. The thick right branch was raised, the thin left one hung down. A very pale moon rose slowly. So did a stranger as they approached the bench.

'Gut yuntif,' he said hoarsely.

Mendel, drained of blood, waved his wasted arms. Isaac yowled sickly. Then a bell chimed and it was only ten. Mendel let out a piercing anguished cry as the bearded stranger disappeared into the bushes. A policeman came running, and though he beat the bushes with his nightstick, could turn up nothing. Mendel and Isaac hurried out of the little park. When Mendel glanced back the dead tree had its thin arm raised, the thick one down. He moaned.

They boarded a trolley, stopping at the home of a former friend, but he had died years ago. On the same block they went into a cafeteria and ordered two fried eggs for Isaac. The tables were crowded except where a heavy-set man sat eating soup with kasha. After one look at him they left in haste, although Isaac wept.

Mendel had another address on a slip of paper but the house was too far away, in Queens, so they stood in a doorway shivering.

What can I do, he frantically thought, in one short hour?

He remembered the furniture in the house. It was junk but might bring a few dollars. 'Come, Isaac.' They went once more to the pawnbroker's to talk to him, but the shop was dark and an iron gate – rings and gold watches glinting through it – was drawn tight across his place of business.

They huddled behind a telephone pole, both freezing. Isaac whimpered.

'See the big moon, Isaac. The whole sky is white.'

He pointed but Isaac wouldn't look.

Mendel dreamed for a minute of the sky lit up, long sheets

of light in all directions. Under the sky, in California, sat Unce Leo drinking tea with lemon. Mendel felt warm but woke up cold.

Across the street stood an ancient brick synagogue.

He pounded on the huge door but no one appeared. He waited till he had breath and desperately knocked again. At last there were footsteps within, and the synagogue door creaked open on its massive brass hinges.

A darkly dressed sexton, holding a dripping candle, glared at them.

'Who knocks this time of night with so much noise on the synagogue door?'

Mendel told the sexton his troubles. 'Please, I would like to speak to the rabbi.'

'The rabbi is an old man. He sleeps now. His wife won't let you see him. Go home and come back tomorrow.'

'To tomorrow I said good-bye already. I am a dying man.'

Though the sexton seemed doubtful he pointed to an old wooden house next door. 'In there he lives.' He disappeared into the synagogue with his lit candle casting shadows around him.

Mendel, with Isaac clutching his sleeve, went up the wooden steps and rang the bell. After five minutes a big-faced, grey-haired bulky woman came out on the porch with a torn robe thrown over her nightdress. She emphatically said the rabbi was sleeping and could not be waked.

But as she was insisting, the rabbi himself tottered to the door. He listened a minute and said, 'Who wants to see me let them come in.'

They entered a cluttered room. The rabbi was an old skinny man with bent shoulders and a wisp of white beard. He wore a flannel nightgown and black skullcap; his feet were bare.

'Vey is mir,' his wife muttered. 'Put on shoes or tomorrow comes sure pneumonia.' She was a woman with a big belly, years younger than her husband. Staring at Isaac, she turned away.

Mendel apologetically related his errand. 'All I need more is thirty-five dollars.'

'Thirty-five?' said the rabbi's wife. 'Why not thirty-five thousand? Who has so much money? My husband is a poor rabbi. The doctors take away every penny.'

'Dear friend,' said the rabbi, 'if I had I would give you.'

'I got already seventy,' Mendel said, heavy-hearted. 'All I need more is thirty-five.'

'God will give you,' said the rabbi.

'In the grave,' said Mendel. 'I need tonight. Come, Isaac.'

'Wait,' called the rabbi.

He hurried inside, came out with a fur-lined caftan, and handed it to Mendel.

'Yascha,' shrieked his wife, 'not your new coat!'

'I got my old one. Who needs two coats for one body?'

'Yascha, I am screaming –'

'Who can go among poor people, tell me, in a new coat?'

'Yascha,' she cried, 'what can this man do with your coat? He needs tonight the money. The pawnbrokers are asleep.'

'So let him wake them up.'

'No.' She grabbed the coat from Mendel.

He held on to a sleeve, wrestling her for the coat. Her I know, Mendel thought. 'Shylock,' he muttered. Her eyes glittered.

The rabbi groaned and tottered dizzily. His wife cried out as Mendel yanked the coat from her hands.

'Run,' cried the rabbi.

'Run, Isaac.'

They ran out of the house and down the steps.

'Stop, you thief,' called the rabbi's wife.

The rabbi pressed both hands to his temples and fell to the floor.

'Help!' his wife wept. 'Heart attack! Help!'

But Mendel and Isaac ran through the streets with the rabbi's new fur-lined caftan. After them noiselessly ran Ginzburg.

It was very late when Mendel bought the train ticket in the only booth open.

There was no time to stop for a sandwich so Isaac ate his peanuts and they hurried to the train in the vast deserted station.

'So in the morning,' Mendel gasped as they ran, 'there comes a man that he sells sandwiches and coffee. Eat but get change. When reaches California the train, will be waiting for you on the station Uncle Leo. If you don't recognize him he will recognize you. Tell him I send best regards.'

But when they arrived at the gate to the platform it was shut, the light out.

Mendel, groaning, beat on the gate with his fists.

'Too late,' said the uniformed ticket collector, a bulky, bearded man with hairy nostrils and a fishy smell.

He pointed to the station clock. 'Already past twelve.'

'But I see standing there still the train,' Mendel said, hopping in his grief.

'It just left – in one more minute.'

'A minute is enough. Just open the gate.'

'Too late I told you.'

Mendel socked his bony chest with both hands. 'With my whole heart I beg you this little favour.'

'Favours you had enough already. For you the train is

gone. You shoulda been dead already at midnight. I told you that yesterday. This is the best I can do.'

'Ginzburg!' Mendel shrank from him.

'Who else?' The voice was metallic, eyes glittered, the expression amused.

'For myself,' the old man begged, 'I don't ask a thing. But what will happen to my boy?'

Ginzburg shrugged lightly. 'What will happen happens. This isn't my responsibility. I got enough to think about without worrying about somebody on one cylinder.'

'What then is your responsibility?'

'To create conditions. To make happen what happens. I ain't in the anthropomorphic business.'

'Whatever business you in, where is your pity?'

'This ain't my commodity. The law is the law.'

'Which law is this?'

'The cosmic universal law, goddamit, the one I got to follow myself.'

'What kind of a law is it?' cried Mendel. 'For God's sake, don't you understand what I went through in my life with this poor boy? Look at him. For thirty-nine years, since the day he was born, I wait for him to grow up, but he don't. Do you understand what this means in a father's heart? Why don't you let him go to his uncle?' His voice had risen and he was shouting.

Isaac mewled loudly.

'Better calm down or you'll hurt somebody's feelings,' Ginzburg said with a wink towards Isaac.

'All my life,' Mendel cried, his body trembling, 'what did I have? I was poor, I suffered from my health. When I worked I worked too hard. When I didn't work was worse. My wife died a young woman. But I didn't ask from anybody nothing. Now I ask a small favour. Be so kind, Mr Ginzburg.'

The ticket collector was picking his teeth with a matchstick.

'You ain't the only one, my friend, some got it worse than you. That's how it goes in this country.'

'You dog you.' Mendel lunged at Ginzburg's throat and began to choke. 'You bastard, don't you understand what it means human?'

They struggled nose to nose, Ginzburg, though his astonished eyes bulged, began to laugh. 'You pipsqueak nothing. I'll freeze you to pieces.'

His eyes lit in rage and Mendel felt an unbearable cold like an icy dagger invading his body, all of his parts shrivelling.

Now I die without helping Isaac.

A crowd gathered. Isaac yelped in fright.

Clinging to Ginzburg in his last agony, Mendel saw reflected in the ticket collector's eyes the depth of his terror. But he saw that Ginzburg, staring at himself in Mendel's eyes, saw mirrored in them the extent of his own awful wrath. He beheld a shimmering, starry, blinding light that produced darkness.

Ginzburg looked astounded. 'Who me?'

His grip on the squirming old man slowly loosened, and Mendel, his heart barely beating, slumped to the ground.

'Go,' Ginzburg muttered, take him to the train.'

'Let pass,' he commanded a guard.

The crowd parted. Isaac helped his father up and they tottered down the steps to the platform where the train waited, lit and ready to go.

Mendel found Isaac a coach seat and hastily embraced him. 'Help Uncle Leo, Isaakil. Also remember your father and mother.'

'Be nice to him,' he said to the conductor. 'Show him where everything is.'

He waited on the platform until the train began slowly to

move. Isaac sat at the edge of his seat, his face strained in the direction of his journey. When the train was gone, Mendel ascended the stairs to see what had become of Ginzburg.

Black Is My Favourite Colour

Charity Sweetness sits in the toilet eating her two hard-boiled eggs while I'm having my ham sandwich and coffee in the kitchen. That's how it goes only don't get the idea of ghettoes. If there's a ghetto I'm the one that's in it. She's my cleaning woman from Father Divine and comes in once a week to my small three-room apartment on my day off from the liquor store. 'Peace,' she says to me, 'Father reached on down and took me right up in Heaven.' She's a small person with a flat body, frizzy hair, and a quiet face that the light shines out of, and Mama had such eyes before she died. The first time Charity Sweetness came in to clean, a little more than a year and a half, I made the mistake to ask her to sit down at the kitchen table with me and eat her lunch. I was still feeling not so hot after Ornita left but I'm the kind of a man – Nat Lime, forty-four, a bachelor with a daily growing bald spot on the back of my head, and I could lose frankly fifteen pounds – who enjoys company so long as he has it. So she cooked up her two hard-boiled eggs and sat down and took a small bite out of one of them. But after a minute she stopped chewing and she got up and carried the eggs in a cup in the bathroom, and since then she eats there. I said to her more than once, 'Okay, Charity Sweetness, so have it your way, eat the eggs in the kitchen by yourself and I'll eat when you're done,' but she smiles absent-minded, and eats in the toilet. It's my fate with coloured people.

Although black is still my favourite colour you wouldn't know it from my luck except in short quantities even though I do all right in the liquor store business in Harlem, on

Eighth Avenue between 110th and 11th. I speak with respect. A large part of my life I've had dealings with Negro people, most on a business basis but sometimes for friendly reasons with genuine feeling on both sides. I'm drawn to them. At this time of my life I should have one or two good coloured friends but the fault isn't necessarily mine. If they knew what was in my heart towards them, but how can you tell that to anybody nowadays? I've tried more than once but the language of the heart either is a dead language or else nobody understands it the way you speak it. Very few. What I'm saying is, personally for me there's only one human colour and that's the colour of blood. I like a black person if not because he's black, then because I'm white. It comes to the same thing. If I wasn't white my first choice would be black. I'm satisfied to be white because I have no other choice. Anyway, I got an eye for colour. I appreciate. Who wants everybody to be the same? Maybe it's like some kind of a talent. Nat Lime might be a liquor dealer in Harlem, but once in the jungle in New Guinea in the Second World War, I got the idea when I shot at a running Jap and missed him, that I had some kind of a talent, though maybe it's the kind where you have a marvellous idea now and then but in the end what do they come to? After all, it's a strange world.

Where Charity Sweetness eats her eggs makes me think about Buster Wilson when we were both boys in the Williamsburg section of Brooklyn. There was this long block of run-down dirty frame houses in the middle of a not-so-hot white neighbourhood full of pushcarts. The Negro houses looked to me like they had been born and died there, dead not long after the beginning of the world. I lived on the next street. My father was a cutter with arthritis in both hands, big red knuckles and swollen fingers so he didn't cut, and my mother was the one who went to work. She sold paper bags from a second-hand pushcart in Ellery Street. We didn't starve but nobody ate chicken unless we were sick or the chicken was. This was my first acquaintance with a lot of black people and I used to poke around on their poor block. I think I thought, brother, if there can be like this, what can't there be ? I mean I caught an early idea what life was about. Anyway I met Buster Wilson there. He used to play marbles by himself. I sat on the kerb across the street, watching him shoot one marble lefty and the other one righty. The hand that won picked up the marbles. It wasn't so much of a game but he didn't ask me to come over. My idea was to be friendly, only he never encouraged, he discouraged. Why did I pick him out for a friend ? Maybe because I had no others then, we were new in the neighbourhood, from Manhattan. Also I liked his type. Buster did everything alone. He was a skinny kid and his brothers' clothes hung on him like worn-out potato sacks. He was a beanpole boy, about twelve, and I was then ten. His arms and legs were burnt out match-sticks. He always wore a brown wool sweater, one arm half unravelled, the other went down to the wrist. His long and narrow head had a white part cut straight in the short woolly hair, maybe with a ruler there, by his father, a barber but too drunk to stay a barber. In those days though I had little myself I was old enough to know who was better off, and the whole block of coloured houses made me feel bad in the daylight. But I went there as much as I could because the street was full of life. In the night it looked different, it's hard to tell a cripple in the dark. Sometimes I was afraid to walk by the houses when they were dark and quiet. I was afraid there were people looking at me that I couldn't see. I liked it better when they had parties at night and everybody had a good time. The musicians played their banjos and saxophones and the houses shook with the music and laughing. The

23

young girls, with their pretty dresses and ribbons in their hair, caught me in my throat when I saw them through the windows.

But with the parties came drinking and fights. Sundays were bad days after the Saturday night parties. I remember once that Buster's father, also long and loose, always wearing a dirty grey Homburg hat, chased another black man in the street with a half-inch chisel. The other one, maybe five feet high, lost his shoe and when they wrestled on the ground he was already bleeding through his suit, a thick red blood smearing the sidewalk. I was frightened by the blood and wanted to pour it back in the man who was bleeding from the chisel. On another time Buster's father was playing in a crap game with two big bouncy red dice, in the back of an alley between two middle houses. Then about six men started fist-fighting there, and they ran out of the alley and hit each other in the street. The neighbours, including children, came out and watched, everybody afraid but nobody moving to do anything. I saw the same thing near my store in Harlem, years later, a big crowd watching two men in the street, their breaths hanging in the air on a winter night, murdering each other with switch knives, but nobody moved to call a cop. I didn't either. Anyway, I was just a young kid but I still remember how the cops drove up in a police paddy wagon and broke up the fight by hitting everybody they could hit with big nightsticks. This was in the days before LaGuardia. Most of the fighters were knocked out cold, only one or two got away. Buster's father started to run back in his house but a cop ran after him and cracked him on his Homburg hat with a club, right on the front porch. Then the Negro men were lifted up by the cops, one at the arms and the other at the feet, and they heaved them in the paddy wagon. Buster's father hit the back of the wagon and fell, with his nose spouting very red blood, on top of three other men. I personally couldn't stand it, I was scared of the human race so I ran home, but I remember Buster watching without any expression in his eyes. I stole an extra fifteen cents from my mother's pocket book and I ran back and asked Buster if he wanted to go to the movies. I would pay. He said yes. This was the first time he talked to me.

So we went more than once to the movies. But we never got to be friends. Maybe because it was a one-way proposition – from me to him. Which includes my invitations to go with me, my (poor mother's) movie money, Hershey chocolate bars, water-melon slices, even my best Nick Carter and Merriwell books that I spent hours picking up in the junk shops, and that he never gave me back. Once he let me go in his house to get a match so we could smoke some butts we found, but it smelled so heavy, so impossible, I died till I got out of there. What I saw in the way of furniture I won't mention – the best was falling apart in pieces. Maybe we went to the movies all together five or six matinées that spring and in the summertime, but when the shows were over he usually walked home by himself.

'Why don't you wait for me, Buster?' I asked. 'We're both going in the same direction.'

But he was walking ahead and didn't hear me. Anyway he didn't answer.

One day when I wasn't expecting it he hit me in the teeth. I felt like crying but not because of the pain. I spit blood and said, 'What did you hit me for? What did I do to you?'

'Because you a Jew bastard. Take your Jew movies and your Jew candy and shove them up your Jew ass.'

And he ran away.

I thought to myself how was I to know he didn't like the movies. When I was a man I thought, you can't force it.

Years later, in the prime of my life, I met Mrs Ornita

Harris. She was standing by herself under an open umbrella at the bus stop, crosstown 110th, and I picked up her green glove that she had dropped on the wet sidewalk. It was in the end of November. Before I could ask her was it hers, she grabbed the glove out of my hand, closed her umbrella, and stepped in the bus. I got on right after her.

I was annoyed so I said, 'If you'll pardon me, Miss, there's no law that you have to say thanks, but at least don't make a criminal out of me.'

'Well, I'm sorry,' she said, 'but I don't like white men trying to do me favours.'

I tipped my hat and that was that. In ten minutes I got off the bus but she was already gone.

Who expected to see her again but I did. She came into my store about a week later for a bottle of scotch.

'I would offer you a discount,' I told her, 'but I know you don't like a certain kind of a favour and I'm not looking for a slap in the face.'

Then she recognized me and got a little embarrassed.

'I'm sorry I misunderstood you that day.'

'So mistakes happen.'

The result was she took the discount. I gave her a dollar off.

She used to come in about every two weeks for a fifth of Haig and Haig. Sometimes I waited on her, sometimes my helpers, Jimmy or Mason, also coloured, but I said to give the discount. They both looked at me but I had nothing to be ashamed. In the spring when she came in we used to talk once in a while. She was a slim woman, dark but not the most dark, about thirty years I would say, also well built, with a combination nice legs and a good-size bosom that I like. Her face was pretty, with big eyes and high cheek bones, big lips a little thick and nose a little broad.

Sometimes she didn't feel like talking, she paid for the bottle, less discount, and walked out. Her eyes were tired and she didn't look to me like a happy woman.

I found out her husband was once a window cleaner on the big buildings, but one day his safety belt broke and he fell fifteen stories. After the funeral she got a job as a manicurist in a Times Square barber shop. I told her I was a bachelor and lived with my mother in a small three-room apartment on West Eighty-third near Broadway. My mother had cancer, and Ornita said she was very sorry.

One night in June we went out together. How that happened I'm still not so sure. I guess I asked her and she didn't say no. Where do you go out with a Negro woman? We went to the Village. We had a good dinner and walked in Washington Square Park. It was a hot night. Nobody was surprised when they saw us, nobody looked at us like we were against the law. If they looked maybe they saw my new lightweight suit that I bought yesterday and my shiny bald spot when we walked under a lamp, also how pretty she was for a man of my type. We went in a movie on West Eighth Street. I didn't want to go in but she said she had heard about the picture. We went in like strangers and we came out like strangers. I wondered what was in her mind and I thought to myself, whatever is in there it's not a certain white man that I know. All night long we went together like we were chained. After the movie she wouldn't let me take her back to Harlem. When I put her in a taxi she asked me, 'Why did we bother?'

For the steak, I wanted to say. Instead I said, 'You're worth the bother.'

'Thanks anyway.'

Kiddo, I thought to myself after the taxi left, you just found out what's what, now the best thing is forget her.

It's easy to say. In August we went out the second time.

That was the night she wore a purple dress and I thought to myself, my God, what colours. Who paints that picture paints a masterpiece. Everybody looked at us but I had pleasure. That night when she took off her dress it was in a furnished room I had the sense to rent a few days before. With my sick mother, I couldn't ask her to come to my apartment, and she didn't want me to go home with her where she lived with her brother's family on West 115th near Lenox Avenue. Under her purple dress she wore a black slip, and when she took that off she had white underwear. When she took off the white underwear she was black again. But I know where the next white was, if you want to call it white. And that was the night I think I fell in love with her, the first time in my life though I have liked one or two nice girls I used to go with when I was a boy. It was a serious proposition. I'm the kind of a man when I think of love I'm thinking of marriage. I guess that's why I am a bachelor.

That same week I had a holdup in my place, two big men – both black – with revolvers. One got excited when I rang open the cash register so he could take the money and he hit me over the ear with his gun. I stayed in the hospital a couple of weeks. Otherwise I was insured. Ornita came to see me. She sat on a chair without talking much. Finally I saw she was uncomfortable so I suggested she ought to go home.

'I'm sorry it happened,' she said.

'Don't talk like it's your fault.'

When I got out of the hospital my mother was dead. She was a wonderful person. My father died when I was thirteen and all by herself she kept the family alive and together. I sat shive for a week and remembered how she sold paper bags on her pushcart. I remembered her life and what she tried to teach me. Nathan, she said, if you ever forget you are a Jew a goy will remind you. Mama, I said, rest in peace

28

on this subject. But if I do something you don't like, remember, on earth its harder than where you are. Then when my week of mourning was finished, one night I said, 'Ornita, let's get married. We're both honest people and if you love me like I love you it won't be such a bad time. If you don't like New York I'll sell out here and we'll move someplace else. Maybe to San Francisco where nobody knows us. I was there for a week in the Second World War and I saw white and coloured living together.'

'Nat,' she answered me, 'I like you but I'd be afraid. My husband woulda killed me.'

'Your husband is dead.'

'Not in my memory.'

'In that case I'll wait.'

'Do you know what it'd be like – I mean the life we could expect?'

'Ornita,' I said, 'I'm the kind of a man, if he picks his own way of life he's satisfied.'

'What about children? Were you looking forward to half-Jewish polka dots?'

'I was looking forward to children.'

'I can't,' she said.

Can't is can't. I saw she was afraid and the best thing was not to push. Sometimes when we met she was so nervous that whatever we did she couldn't enjoy it. At the same time I still thought I had a chance. We were together more and more. I got rid of my furnished room and she came to my apartment – I gave away Mama's bed and bought a new one. She stayed with me all day on Sundays. When she wasn't so nervous she was affectionate, and if I know what love is, I had it. We went out a couple of times a week, the same way – usually I met her in Times Square and sent her home in a taxi, but I talked more about marriage and she talked less against it. One night she told me she was still trying to convince herself but she was almost convinced. I took an inventory of my liquor stock so I could put the store up for sale.

Ornita knew what I was doing. One day she quit her job, the next she took it back. She also went away a week to visit her sister in Philadelphia for a little rest. She came back tired but said maybe. Maybe is maybe so I'll wait. The way she said it it was closer to yes. That was the winter two years ago. When she was in Philadelphia I called up a friend of mine from the Army, now a CPA, and told him I would appreciate an invitation for an evening. He knew why. His wire said yes right away. When Ornita came back we went there. The wife made a fine dinner. It wasn't a bad time and they told us to come again. Ornita had a few drinks. She looked relaxed, wonderful. Later, because of a twenty-four hour strike I had to take her home on the subway. When we got to the 116th Street station she told me to stay on the train, and she would walk the couple of blocks to her house. I didn't like a woman walking alone on the street at that time of the night. She said she never had any trouble but I insisted nothing doing. I said I would walk to her stoop with her and when she went upstairs I would go back to the subway.

On the way there, on 115th in the middle of the block before Lenox, we were stopped by three men – maybe they were boys. One had a black hat with a half-inch brim, one a green cloth hat, and the third wore a black leather cap. The green hat was wearing a short coat and the other two had long ones. It was under a street light but the leather cap snapped a six-inch switchblade open in the light.

'What you doin' with this white son of a bitch?' he said to Ornita.

'I'm minding my own business,' she answered him, 'and I wish you would too.'

'Boys,' I said, 'we're all brothers. I'm a reliable merchant in the neighbourhood. This young lady is my dear friend. We don't want any trouble. Please let us pass.'

'You talk like a Jew landlord,' said the green hat. 'Fifty a week for a single room.'

'No charge for the rats,' said the half-inch brim.

'Believe me, I'm no landlord. My store is "Nathan's Liquors" between Hundred Tenth and Eleventh. I also have two coloured clerks, Mason and Jimmy, and they will tell you I pay good wages as well as I give discounts to certain customers.'

'Shut your mouth, Jewboy,' said the leather cap, and he moved the knife back and forth in front of my coat button. 'No more black pussy for you.'

'Speak with respect about this lady, please.'

I got slapped on my mouth.

'That ain't no lady,' said the long face in the half-inch brim, 'that's black pussy. She deserve to have evvy bit of her hair shave off. How you like to have evvy bit of your hair shave off, black pussy?'

'Please leave me and this gentleman alone or I'm gonna scream long and loud. That's my house three doors down.'

They slapped her. I never heard such a scream. Like her husband was falling fifteen stories.

I hit the one that slapped her and the next I knew I was laying in the gutter with a pain in my head. I thought, goodbye, Nat, they'll stab me for sure, but all they did was take my wallet and run in three different directions.

Ornita walked back with me to the subway and she wouldn't let me go home with her again.

'Just get home safely.'

She looked terrible. Her face was grey and I still remembered her scream. It was a terrible winter night, very cold

February, and it took me an hour and ten minutes to get home. I felt bad for leaving her but what could I do?

We had a date downtown the next night but she didn't show up, the first time.

In the morning I called her in her place of business.

'For God's sake, Ornita, if we got married and moved away we wouldn't have that kind of trouble that we had. We wouldn't come in that neighbourhood any more.'

'Yes, we would. I have family there and don't want to move anyplace else. The truth of it is I can't marry you, Nat. I got troubles enough of my own.'

'I coulda sworn you love me.'

'Maybe I do but I can't marry you.'

'For God's sake, why?'

'I got enough trouble of my own.'

I went that night in a cab to her brother's house to see her. He was a quiet man with a thin moustache. 'She gone,' he said, 'left for a long visit to some close relatives in the South. She said to tell you she appreciate your intentions but didn't think it will work out.'

'Thank you kindly,' I said.

Don't ask me how I got home.

Once on Eighth Avenue, a couple of blocks from my store, I saw a blind man with a white cane tapping on the sidewalk. I figured we were going in the same direction so I took his arm.

'I can tell you're white,' he said.

A heavy coloured woman with a full shopping bag rushed after us.

'Never mind,' she said, 'I know where he live.'

She pushed me with her shoulder and I hurt my leg on the fire hydrant.

That's how it is. I give my heart and they kick me in my teeth.

'Charity Sweetness – you hear me? – come out of that goddamn toilet!'

Still Life

Months after vainly seeking a studio on the vie Margutta, del Babuino, della Croce, and elsewhere in that neighbourhood, Arthur Fidelman settled for part of a crowded windowy, attic-like atelier on a cobblestone street in the Trastevere, strung high with sheets and underwear. He had, a week before, in 'personal notices' in the American language newspaper in Rome, read: 'Studio to share, cheap, many advantages, etc., A. Oliovino,' and after much serious anguish (the curt advertisement having recalled dreams he had dreamed were dead), many indecisions, enunciations and renunciations, Fidelman had, one very cold late-December morning, hurried to the address given, a worn four-storey building with a yellowish façade stained brown along the edges. On the top floor, in a thickly cluttered artist's studio smelling aromatically of turpentine and oil paints, the inspiring sight of an easel lit in unwavering light from the three large windows setting the former art student on fire once more to paint, he had dealt not with a pittore, as expected, but with a pittrice, Annamaria Oliovino.

The pittrice, a thin, almost gaunt, high-voiced, restless type, with short black uncombed hair, violet mouth, distracted eyes and tense neck, a woman with narrow buttocks and piercing breasts, was in her way attractive if not in truth beautiful. She had on a thick black woollen sweater, eroded black velveteen culottes, black socks, and leather sandals spotted with drops of paint. Fidelman and she eyed each other stealthily and he realized at once she was, as a woman, indifferent to him or his type, who or which made no difference. But after ten minutes, despite the turmoil she exuded even as she dispassionately answered his hesitant questions, the art student, ever a sucker for strange beauty and all sorts of experiences, felt himself involved with and falling for her. Not my deep dish, he warned himself, aware of all the dangers to him and his renewed desire to create art; yet he was already half in love with her. It can't be, he thought in desperation; but it could. It had happened to him before. In her presence he tightly shut both eyes and wholeheartedly wished against what might be. Really he trembled, and though he laboured to extricate his fate from hers, he was already a plucked bird, greased, and ready for frying. Fidelman protested within – cried out severely against the weak self, called himself ferocious names but could do not much, a victim of his familiar response, a too passionate fondness for strangers. So Annamaria, who had advertised a twenty thousand lire monthly rental, in the end doubled the sum, and Fidelman paid through both nostrils, cash for first and last months (should he attempt to fly by night) plus a deposit of ten thousand for possible damages. An hour later he moved in with his imitation leather suitcase. This happened in the dead of winter. Below the cold sunlit windows stood two frozen umbrella pines and beyond, in the near distance, sparkled the icy Tiber.

The studio was well heated, Annamaria had insisted, but the cold leaked in through the wide windows. It was more a blast; the art student shivered but was kept warm by his hidden love for the pittrice. It took him most of a day to clear himself a space to work, about a third of the studio was as much as he could manage. He stacked her canvases five deep against her portion of the walls, curious to examine them, but Annamaria watched his every move (he noticed several self-portraits) although she was at the same time painting a monumental natura morta of a loaf of bread with

35

two garlic bulbs ('Pane ed Aglii'). He moved stacks of *Oggi*, piles of postcards and yellowed letters, and a bundle of calendars going back to many years ago; also a Perugina candy box full of broken pieces of Etruscan pottery, one of small sea shells, and a third of medallions of various saints and of the Virgin, which she warned him to handle with care. He had uncovered a sagging cot by a dripping stone sink in his corner of the studio and there he slept. She furnished an old chafing dish and a broken table, and he bought a few household things he needed. Annamaria rented the art student an easel for a thousand lire a month. Her quarters were private, a room at the other end of the studio whose door she kept locked, handing him the key when he had to use the toilet. The wall was thin and the instrument noisy. He could hear the whistle and rush of her water, and though he tried to be quiet, because of the plumbing the bowl was always brimful and the pour of his stream embarrassed him. At night, if there was need, although he was tempted to use the sink, he fished out the yellowed, sedimented pot under his bed; once or twice, as he was using it in the thick of night, he had the impression she was awake and listening.

They painted in their overcoats, Annamaria wearing a black babushka, Fidelman a green wool hat pulled down over his frozen ears. She kept a pan of hot coals at her feet and every so often lifted a sandalled foot to toast it. The marble floor of the studio was sheer thick ice; Fidelman wore two pairs of tennis socks his sister Bessie had recently sent from the States. Annamaria, a leftie, painted with a smeared leather glove on her hand, and theoretically his easel had been arranged so that he couldn't see what she was doing but he often sneaked looks at her work. The pittrice, to his surprise, painted with flicks of her fingers and wrists, peering at her performance with almost shut eyes. He noticed she alternated still lifes with huge lyric abstractions – massive whorls of red and gold exploding in all directions, these built on, entwined with, and ultimately concealing a small black religious cross, her first two brush strokes on every abstract canvas. Once when Fidelman gathered the nerve to ask her why the cross, she answered it was the symbol that gave the painting its meaning.

He was eager to know more but she was impatient. 'Eh,' she shrugged, 'who can explain art?'

Though her response to his various attempts to become better acquainted were as a rule curt, and her voluntary attention to him shorter still – she was able, apparently, to pretend he wasn't there – Fidelman's feeling for Annamaria grew, and he was as unhappy in love as he had ever been.

But he was patient, a persistent virtue, served her often in various capacities, for instance carrying down four flights of stairs her two bags of garbage shortly after supper – the portinaia was crippled and the portiere never around – sweeping the studio clean each morning, even running to retrieve a brush or paint tube when she happened to drop one – offering any service any time, you name it. She accepted these small favours without giving them notice.

One morning after reading a many-paged letter she had just got in the mail, Annamaria was sad, sullen, unable to work; she paced around restlessly, it troubled him. But after feverishly painting a widening purple spiral that continued off the canvas, she regained a measure of repose. This heightened her beauty, lent it somehow a youthful quality it didn't ordinarily have – he guessed her to be no older than twenty-seven or -eight; so Fidelman, inspired by the change in her, hoping it might foretoken better luck for him, approached Annamaria, removed his hat and suggested since she went out infrequently why not lunch for a change at the trattoria at the corner, Guido's, where workmen assembled

and the veal and white wine were delicious? She, to his surprise, after darting an uneasy glance out of the window at
the tops of the motionless umbrella pines, abruptly assented.
They ate well and conversed like human beings, although
she mostly limited herself to answering his modest questions.
She informed Fidelman she had come from Naples to Rome
two years ago, although it seemed much longer, and he told
her he was from the United States. Being so physically close
to her, able to inhale the odour of her body – like salted
flowers – and intimately eating together, excited Fidelman,
and he sat very still, not to rock the boat and spill a drop of
what was so precious to him. Annamaria ate hungrily, her
eyes usually lowered. Once she looked at him with a shade of
a smile and he felt beatitude; the art student contemplated
many such meals though he could ill afford them, every cent
he spent, saved and sent by Bessie.

After zuppa inglese and a peeled apple she patted her lips
with a napkin, and still in good humour, suggested they take
the bus to the Piazza del Popolo and visit some painter
friends of hers.

'I'll introduce you to Alberto Moravia.'

'With pleasure,' Fidelman said, bowing.

But when they stepped into the street and were walking
to the bus stop near the river a cold wind blew up and
Annamaria turned pale.

'Something wrong?' Fidelman inquired.

'The East Wind,' she answered testily.

'What wind?'

'The Evil Eye,' she said with irritation. 'Malocchio.'

He had heard something of the sort. They returned
quickly to the studio, their heads lowered against the noisy
wind, the pittrice from time to time furtively crossing herself.
A black-habited old nun passed them at the trattoria corner,
from whom Annamaria turned in torment, muttering,

'Jettatura! Porca miseria!' When they were upstairs in the studio she insisted Fidelman touch his testicles three times to undo or dispel who knows what witchcraft, and he modestly obliged. Her request had inflamed him although he cautioned himself to remember it was, in purpose and essence, theological.

Later she received a visitor, a man who came to see her on Monday and Friday afternoons after his work in a government bureau. Her visitors, always men, whispered with her a minute, then left restlessly; most of them, excepting also Giancarlo Balducci, a crosseyed illustrator – Fidelman never saw again. But the one who came oftenest stayed longest, a solemn grey-haired gent, Augusto Ottogalli, with watery blue eyes and missing side teeth, old enough to be her father for sure. He wore a slanted black fedora, and a shabby grey overcoat too large for him, greeted Fidelman vacantly and made him inordinately jealous. When Augusto arrived in the afternoon the pittrice usually dropped anything she was doing and they retired to her room, at once locked and bolted. The art student wandered alone in the studio for dreadful hours. When Augusto ultimately emerged, looking dishevelled, and if successful, defeated, Fidelman turned his back on him and the old man hastily let himself out of the door. After his visits, and only his, Annamaria did not appear in the studio for the rest of the day. Once when Fidelman knocked on her door to invite her out to supper, she told him to use the pot because she had a headache and was sound asleep. On another occasion when Augusto was locked long in her room with her, after a tormenting two hours Fidelman tiptoed over and put his jealous ear to the door. All he could hear was the buzz and sigh of their whispering. Peeking through the keyhole he saw them both in their overcoats, sitting on her bed, Augusto tightly clasping her hands, whispering passionately, his nose empurpled with emotion,

Annamaria's white face averted. When the art student checked an hour afterward, they were still at it, the old man imploring, the pittrice weeping. The next time, Augusto came with a priest, a portly, heavy-breathing man with a doubtful face. But as soon as they appeared in the studio Annamaria, enraged to fury, despite the impassioned entreatments of Augusto, began to throw at them anything of hers or Fidelman's she could lay hands on.

'Bloodsuckers!' she shouted, 'scorpions! parasites!' until they had hastily retreated. Yet when Augusto, worn and harried, returned alone, without complaint she retired to her room with him.

2

Fidelman's work, despite the effort and despair he gave it, was going poorly. Every time he looked at unpainted canvas he saw harlequins, whores, tragic kings, fragmented musicians, the sick and the dread. Still, tradition was tradition and what if he should want to make more? Since he had always loved art history he considered embarking on a 'Mother and Child', but was afraid her image would come out too much Bessie – after all, fifteen years between them. Or maybe a moving 'Pietà', the dead son's body held like a broken wave in mama's frail arms? A curse on art history – he fought the fully prefigured picture though some of his former best paintings had jumped in every detail to the mind. Yet if so, where's true engagement? Sometimes I'd like to forget every picture I've seen, Fidelman thought. Almost in panic he sketched in charcoal a coat-tailed 'Figure of a Jew Fleeing' and quickly hid it away. After that, ideas, prefigured or not, were scarce. 'Astonish me,' he muttered to himself, wondering whether to return to surrealism. He also considered a series of 'Relations to Place and Space', constructions in squares and circles, the pleasures of tri-dimensional geometry or linear abstraction, only he had little heart for it. The furthest abstraction Fidelman thought, is the blank canvas. A moment later he asked himself, if painting shows who you are, why should not painting?

After the incident with the priest Annamaria was despondent for a week, stayed in her room sometimes bitterly crying, Fidelman often standing helplessly by her door. However this was a prelude to a burst of creativity by the pittrice. Works by the dozens leaped from her brush and stylus. She continued her lyric abstractions based on the theme of a hidden cross and spent hours with a long black candle, burning holes in heavy white paper ('Buchi Spontanei'). Having mixed coffee grounds, sparkling bits of crushed mirror and ground-up sea shells, she blew the dust on mucilaged paper ('Velo nella Nebbia'). She composed collages of rags and toilet tissue. After a dozen linear studies ('Linee Discendenti'), she experimented with gold leaf sprayed with umber, the whole while wet combed in long undulations with a fine comb. She framed this in a black frame and hung it on end like a diamond ('Luce di Candela'). Annamaria worked intently, her brow furrowed, violet mouth tightly pursed, eyes lit, nostrils palpitating in creative excitement. And when she had temporarily run out of new ideas she did a mythological bull in red clay ('La Donna Toro'), afterwards returning to nature morte with bunches of bananas; then self-portraits.

The pittrice occasionally took time out to see what Fidelman was up to, although not much, and then editing his efforts. She changed lines and altered figures, or swabbed paint over whole compositions that didn't appeal to her. There was not much that did, but Fidelman was grateful for any attention she gave his work, and even kept at it to incite her criticism. He could feel his heart beat in his teeth whenever she stood close to him modifying his work, he deeply breathing her intimate smell of sweating flowers. She used perfume only when Augusto came and it disappointed Fidelman that the old man should evoke the use of bottled fragrance; yet he was cheered that her natural odour which he, so to say, got for free, was so much more exciting than the stuff she doused herself with for her decrepit Romeo. He had noticed she had a bit of soft belly but he loved the pliant roundness and often daydreamed of it. Thinking it might please her, for he pleased her rarely (he reveried how it would be once she understood the true depth of his love for her), the art student experimented with some of the things Annamaria had done – the spontaneous holes, for instance, several studies of 'Lines Ascending', and two lyrical abstract expressionistic pieces based on, interwoven with, and ultimately concealing a Star of David, although for these attempts he soon discovered he had earned, instead of her good will, an increased measure of scorn.

However, Annamaria continued to eat lunch with him at Guido's, and more often than not, supper, although she said practically nothing during meals and afterwards let her eye roam over the faces of the men at the other tables. But there were times after they had eaten when she would agree to go for a short walk with Fidelman, if there was no serious wind; and once in a while they entered a movie in the Trastevere for she hated to cross any of the bridges of the Tiber, and then only in a bus, sitting stiffly, staring ahead. As they were once riding, Fidelman seized the opportunity to hold her tense fist in his, but as soon as they were across the river she tore it out of his grasp. He was by now giving her presents – tubes of paints, the best brushes, a few yards of Belgian linen, which she accepted without comment; she also borrowed small sums from him, nothing startling – a hundred lire today, five hundred tomorrow. And she announced one morning that he would thereafter, since he used so much of both, have to pay additional for water and electricity – he already paid extra for the heatless heat. Fidelman, though continually worried about money, assented. He would have given his last lira to lie on her soft belly, but she offered niente, not so much as a caress; until one day, he was permitted to look on as she sketched herself nude in his presence. Since it was bitter cold the pittrice did this in two stages. First she removed her sweater and brassiere, and viewing herself in a long, faded mirror, quickly sketched the upper half of her body before it turned blue. He was dizzily enamoured of her form and flesh. Hastily fastening the brassiere and pulling on her sweater, Annamaria stepped out of her sandals and peeled off her culottes, and white panties torn at the crotch, then drew the rest of herself down to her toes. The art student begged permission to sketch along with her but the pittrice denied it, so he had, as best one can, to commit to memory her lovely treasures – the hard, piercing breasts, narrow shapely buttocks, vine-hidden labis, the font and sweet beginning of time. After she had drawn herself and dressed, and when Augusto appeared and they had retired behind her bolted door, Fidelman sat motionless on his high stool before the glittering blue-skied windows, slowly turning to ice to faint strains of Bach.

3

The art student increased his services to Annamaria, her increase was scorn, or so it seemed. This severely bruised his spirit. What have I done to deserve such treatment? That I pay my plenty of rent on time? That I buy her all sorts of presents, not to mention two full meals a day? That I live in flaming hot and freezing cold? That I passionately adore each sweet-and-sour bit of her? He figured it bored her to see so much of him. For a week Fidelman disappeared during the day, sat in cold libraries or stood around in frosty museums. He tried painting after midnight and into the early morning hours but the pittrice found out and unscrewed the bulbs before she went to bed. 'Don't waste my electricity, this isn't America.' He screwed in a dim blue bulb and worked silently from one a.m to five. At dawn he discovered he had painted a blue picture. Fidelman wandered in the streets of the city. At night he slept in the studio and could hear her sleeping in her room. She slept restlessly, dreamed badly, and often moaned. He dreamed he had three eyes.

For two weeks he spoke to no one but a dumpy four-and-a half-foot female on the third floor, and to her usually to say no. Fidelman, having often heard the music of Bach drifting up from below, had tried to picture the lady piano player, imagining a quiet blonde with a slender body, a woman of grace and beauty. It had turned out to be Clelia Monte- maggio, a middle-aged old maid music teacher, who sat at an old upright piano, her apartment door open to let out the cooking smells, particularly fried fish on Friday. Once when coming up from bringing down the garbage, Fidelman had paused to listen to part of a partita at her door and she had lassoed him in for an espresso and pastry. He ate and listened to Bach, her plump bottom moving spryly on the bench as she played not badly. 'Lo spirito,' she called to him raptly over her shoulder, 'l'architettura!' Fidelman nodded. Thereafter whenever she spied him in the hall she attempted to entice him with cream-filled pastries and J.S.B., whom she played apparently exclusively.

'Come een,' she called in English, 'I weel play for you.

We weel talk. There is no use for too much solitude.' But the art student, burdened by his, spurned hers.

Unable to work, he wandered in the streets in a desolate mood, his spirit dusty in a city of fountains and leaky water taps. Water, water everywhere, spouting, flowing, dripping, whispering secrets, love love love, but not for him. If Rome's so sexy, where's mine? Fidelman's Romeless Rome. It belonged least to those who yearned most for it. With slow steps he climbed the Pincio, if possible to raise his spirits gazing down at the rooftops of the city, spires, cupolas, towers, monuments, compounded history and past time. It was in sight, possessable, all but its elusive spirit; after so long he was still straniero. He was then struck by a thought: if you could paint this sight, give it its quality in yours, the spirit belonged to you. History become aesthetic! Fidelman's scalp thickened. A wild rush of things he might paint swept sweetly through him: saints in good and bad health, whole or maimed, in gold and red; nude grey rabbis at Auschwitz, black or white Negroes – what not when *any* colour dripped from your brush? And if these, so also ANNAMARIA ES PULCHRA. He all but cheered. What more intimate possession of a woman! He would paint her, whether she permitted or not, posed or not – she was his to paint, he could with eyes shut. Maybe something will come after all of my love for her. His spirits elevated, Fidelman ran most of the way home.

It took him eight days, a labour of love. He tried her as nude and although able to imagine every inch of her, could not commit it to canvas. Then he suffered until it occurred to him to paint her as 'Virgin with Child'. The idea astonished and elated him. Fidelman went feverishly to work and caught an immediate likeness in paint. Annamaria, saintly beautiful, held in her arms the infant resembling his little nephew Georgie. The pittrice, aware, of course, of his continuous activity, cast curious glances his way, but Fidelman, painting in the corner by the stone sink, kept the easel turned away from her. She pretended unconcern. Done for the day he covered the painting and carefully guarded it. The art student was painting Annamaria in a passion of tenderness for the infant at her breast, her face responsive to its innocence. When, on the ninth day, in trepidation Fidelman revealed his work, the pittrice's eyes clouded and her underlip curled. He was about to grab the canvas and smash it up all over the place when her expression fell apart. The art student postponed all movement but visible trembling. She seemed at first appalled, a darkness descended on her, she was undone. She wailed wordlessly, then sobbed, 'You have seen my soul.' They embraced tempestuously, her breasts stabbing him. Annamaria bawling on his shoulder. Fidelman kissed her wet face and salted lips, she murmuring as he fooled with the hook of her brassiere under her sweater, 'Aspetta, aspetta, caro, Augusto viene.' He was mad with expectation and suspense.

Augusto, who usually arrived punctually at four, did not appear that Friday afternoon. Uneasy as the hour approached, Annamaria seemed relieved as the streets grew dark. She had worked badly after viewing Fidelman's painting, smiled frequently, gazed at him with sweet-sad smiles. At six she gave in to his urging and they retired to her room, his unframed 'Virgin with Child' already hanging above her bed, replacing a gaunt self-portrait. He was curiously disappointed in the picture – surfacy thin – and made a mental note to borrow it back in the morning to work on it more. But the conception, at least, deserved the reward. Annamaria cooked supper. She cut his meat for him and fed him forkfuls. She peeled Fidelman's orange and stirred sugar in his coffee. Afterwards, at his nod, she locked and bolted the studio and bedroom doors and they undressed and slipped under her blankets. How good to be for a change on this side of the locked door, Fidelman thought, relaxing marvellously. Annamaria, however, seemed tensely alert to the noises of the old building, including a parrot screeching, some shouting kids running up the stairs, a soprano singing 'Ritorna, vincitor!' But she calmed down and then hotly embraced Fidelman. In the middle of a passionate kiss the doorbell rang.

Annamaria stiffened in his arms. 'Diavolo! Augusto!'

'He'll go away,' Fidelman advised. 'Both doors locked.'

But she was at once out of bed, drawing on her culottes. 'Get dressed,' she said.

He hopped up and hastily got into his pants.

Annamaria unlocked and unbolted the inner door and then the outer one. It was the postman waiting to collect ten lire for an overweight letter from Naples.

After she had read the long letter and wiped away a tear they undressed and got back into bed.

'Who is he to you?' Fidelman asked.

'Who?'

'Augusto.'

'An old friend. Like a father. We went through much together.'

'Were you lovers?'

'Look, if you want me, take me. If you want to ask questions, go back to school.'

He determined to mind his business.

'Warm me,' she said, 'I'm freezing.'

Fidelman stroked her slowly. After ten minutes she said, '"Gioco di mano, gioco di villano." Use your imagination.'

He used his imagination and she responded with excitement. 'Dolce tesoro,' she whispered, flicking the tip of her tongue into his ear, then with little bites biting his ear lobe.

The doorbell rang loudly.

'For Christ's sake, don't answer,' Fidelman groaned. He tried to hold her down but she was already up, hunting her robe.

'Put on your pants,' she hissed.

He had thoughts of waiting for her in bed but it ended with his dressing fully. She sent him to the door. It was the crippled portinaia, the art student having neglected to take down the garbage.

Annamaria furiously got the two bags and handed them to her.

In bed she was so cold her teeth chattered.

Tense with desire Fidelman warmed her.

'Angelo mio,' she murmured. 'Amore, possess me.'

He was about to when she rose in a hurry. 'The cursed door again!'

Fidelman gnashed his teeth. 'I heard nothing.'

In her torn yellow silk robe she hurried to the front door, opened and shut it, quickly locked and bolted it, did the same in her room and slid into bed.

'You were right, it was nobody.'

She embraced him, her hairy armpits perfumed. He responded with postponed passion.

'Enough of antipasto,' Annamaria said. She reached for his member.

Overwrought, Fidelman though fighting himself not to, spent himself in her hand. Although he mightily willed resurrection, his wilted flower bit the dust.

She furiously shoved him out of bed, into the studio, flinging his clothes after him.

'Pig, beast, onanist!'

4

At least she lets me love her. Daily Fidelman shopped, cooked, and cleaned for her. Every morning he took her shopping sack off the hook, went to the street market and returned with the bag stuffed full of greens, pasta, eggs, meat, cheese, wine, bread. Annamaria insisted on three hearty meals a day although she had once told him she no longer enjoyed eating. Twice he had seen her throw up her supper. What she enjoyed he didn't know except it wasn't Fidelman. After he had served her at her table he was allowed to eat alone in the studio. At two every afternoon she took her siesta, and though it was forbidden to make noise, he was allowed to wash the dishes, dust and clean her room, swab the toilet bowl. She called, Fatso, and in he trotted to get her anything she had run out of – drawing pencils, sanitary belt, safety pins. After she waked from her nap, rain or shine, snow or hail, he was now compelled to leave the studio so she could work in peace and quiet. He wandered, in the tramontana, from one cold two-bit movie to another. At seven he was back to prepare her supper, and twice a week Augusto's, who sported a new black hat and spiffy overcoat, and pitied the art student with both wet blue eyes but wouldn't look at him. After supper, another load of dishes, the garbage downstairs, and when Fidelman returned, with or without Augusto Annamaria was already closeted behind her bolted door. He checked through the keyhole on Mondays and Fridays but she and the old gent were fully clothed. Fidelman had more than once complained to her that his punishment exceeded his crime, but the pittrice said he was a type she would never have any use for. In fact he did not exist for her. Not existing how could he paint,

49

although he told himself he must ? He couldn't. He aimlessly froze wherever he went, a mean cold that seared his lungs, although under his overcoat he wore a new thick sweater Bessie had knitted for him, and two woollen scarves around his neck. Since the night Annamaria had kicked him out of bed he had not been warm; yet he often dreamed of ultimate victory. Once when he was on his lonely way out of the house – a night she was giving a party for some painter friends, Fidelman, a drooping butt in the corner of his mouth, carrying the garbage bags, met Clelia Montemaggio coming up the stairs.

'You look like a frozen board,' she said. 'Come in and enjoy the warmth and a little Bach.'

Unable to unfreeze enough to say no, he continued down with the garbage.

'Every man gets the woman he deserves,' she called after him.

'Who got,' Fidelman muttered. 'Who gets.'

He considered jumping into the Tiber but it was full of ice that winter.

One night at the end of February, Annamaria, to Fidelman's astonishment – it deeply affected him – said he might go with her to a party at Giancarlo Balducci's studio on the Via dell'Occa; she needed somebody to accompany her in the bus across the bridge and Augusto was flat on his back with the Asian flu. The party was lively – painters, sculptors, some writers, two diplomats, a prince and a visiting Hindu sociologist, their ladies and three hotsy-totsy, scantily dressed, unattached girls. One of them, a shapely beauty with orange hair, bright eyes, and warm ways became interested in Fidelman, except that he was dazed by Annamaria, seeing her in a dress for the first time, a ravishing, rich, ruby-coloured affair. The crosseyed host had provided simply a huge cut-glass bowl of spiced mulled wine, and the guests dipped ceramic glasses into it, and guzzled away. Everyone but the art student seemed to be enjoying himself. One or two of the men disappeared into other rooms with female friends or acquaintances and Annamaria, in a gay mood, did a fast shimmy to rhythmic handclapping. She was drinking steadily and when she wanted her glass filled, politely called him 'Arturo'. He began to have mild thoughts of possibly possessing her.

The party bloomed, at least forty, and turned wildish. Practical jokes were played. Fidelman realized his left shoe had been smeared with mustard. Balducci's black cat mewed at a fat lady's behind, a slice of sausage pinned to her dress. Before midnight there were two fist-fights, Fidelman enjoying both but not getting involved, though once he was socked on the neck by a sculptor who had aimed at a painter. The girl with the orange hair, still interested in the art student, invited him to join her in Balducci's bedroom, but he continued to be devoted to Annamaria, his eyes tied to her every move. He was jealous of the illustrator, who whenever near her, nipped her bottom.

One of the sculptors, Orazio Pinelli, a slender man with a darkish face, heavy black brows, and bleached blond hair approached Fidelman. 'Haven't we met before, caro?'

'Maybe,' the art student said, perspiring lightly. 'I'm Arthur Fidelman, an American painter.'

'You don't say? Action painter?'

'Always active.'

'I refer of course to Abstract Expressionism.'

'Of course. Well, sort of. On and off.'

'Haven't I seen some of your work around? Galleria Schneider? Some symmetric, hard-edge, biomorphic forms? Not bad as I remember.'

Fidelman thanked him, in full blush.

'Who are you here with?' Orazio Pinelli asked.

'Annamaria Oliovino.'

'Her?' said the sculptor. 'But she's a fake.'

'Is she?' Fidelman said with a sigh.

'Have you looked at her work?'

'With one eye. Her art is bad but I find her irresistible.'

'Peccato.' The sculptor shrugged and drifted away.

A minute later there was another fist-fight, during which the bright-eyed orange head conked Fidelman with a Chinese vase. He went out cold and when he came to, Annamaria and Balducci were undressing him in the illustrator's bedroom. Fidelman experienced an almost overwhelming pleasure, then Balducci explained that the art student had been chosen to pose in the nude for drawings both he and the pittrice would do of him. He explained there had been a discussion as to which of them did male nudes best and they had decided to settle it in a short contest. Two easels had been wheeled to the centre of the studio; a half hour was allotted to the contestants, and the guests would judge who had done the better job. Though he at first objected because it was a cold night, Fidelman nevertheless felt warmish from wine so he agreed to pose; besides he was proud of his muscles and maybe if she sketched him nude it might arouse her interest for a tussle later. And if he wasn't painting he was at least being painted.

So the pittrice and Giancarlo Balducci, in paint-smeared smocks, worked for thirty minutes by the clock, the whole party silently looking on, with the exception of the orange-haired tart, who sat in the corner eating a prosciutto sandwich. Annamaria, her brow furrowed, lips pursed, drew intensely with crayon; Balducci worked calmly in coloured chalk. The guests were absorbed, although after ten minutes the Hindu went home. A journalist locked himself in the painter's bedroom with orange head and would not admit his wife who pounded on the door. Fidelman, standing barefoot on a bathmat, was eager to see what Annamaria was accomplishing but had to be patient. When the half hour was up he was permitted to look. Balducci had drawn a flock of green and black abstract testiculate circles. Fidelman shuddered. But Annamaria's drawing was representational, not Fidelman although of course inspired by him: A gigantic funereal phallus that resembled a broken-backed snake. The blond sculptor inspected it with half-closed eyes, then yawned and left. By now the party was over, the guests departed, lights out except for a few dripping white candles. Balducci was collecting his ceramic glasses and emptying ash-trays, and Annamaria had thrown up. The art student afterwards heard her begging the illustrator to sleep with her but Balducci complained of fatigue.

'I will if he won't,' Fidelman offered.

Annamaria, enraged, spat on her picture of his unhappy phallus.

'Don't dare come near me,' she cried. 'Malocchio! Jettatura!'

5

The next morning he awoke sneezing, a nasty cold. How can I go on? Annamaria, showing no signs of pity or remorse, continued shrilly to berate him. 'You've brought me nothing but bad luck since you came here. I'm letting you stay because you pay well but I warn you to keep out of my sight.'

'But how –' he asked hoarsely.

'That doesn't concern me.'

'– how will I paint?'

'Who cares? Paint at night.'

'Without light –'

'Paint in the dark. I'll buy you a can of black paint.'

53

'How can you be so cruel to a man who loves –'

'I'll scream,' she said.

He left in anguish. Later while she was at her siesta he came back, got some of his things and tried to paint in the hall. No dice. Fidelman wandered in the rain. He sat for hours on the Spanish Steps. Then he returned to the house and went slowly up the stairs. The door was locked. 'Annamaria,' he hoarsely called. Nobody answered. In the street he stood at the river wall, watching the dome of St Peter's in the distance. Maybe a potion, Fidelman thought, or an amulet? He doubted either would work. How did you go about hanging yourself? In the late afternoon he went back to the house – would say he was sick, needed rest, possibly a doctor. He felt feverish. She could hardly refuse.

But she did, although explaining she felt bad herself. He held on to the banister as he went down the stairs. Clelia Montemaggio's door was open. Fidelman paused, then continued down but she had seen him. 'Come een, come een.'

He went reluctantly in. She fed him camomile tea and panettone. He ate in a wolfish hurry as she seated herself at the piano.

'No Bach, please, my head aches from various troubles.'

'Where's your dignity?' she asked.

'Try Chopin, that's lighter.'

'Respect yourself, please.'

Fidelman removed his hat as she began to play a Bach prelude, her bottom rhythmic on the bench. Though his cold oppressed him and he could hardly breathe, tonight the spirit, the architecture, moved him. He felt his face to see if he was crying but only his nose was wet. On the top of the piano Clelia had paced a bowl of white carnations in full bloom. Each white petal seemed a white flower. If I could paint those gorgeous flowers, Fidelman thought. If I could

I was confused and threw it into the Tiber. I was afraid it
was an idiot.'

She was sobbing. He drew back.

'Wait,' she wept. 'The next time in bed Augusto was im-
potent. Since then he's been imploring me to confess so he
can get back his powers. But every time I step into the con-
fessional my tongue turns to bone. The priest can't tear a
word out of me. That's how it's been all my life, don't ask
me why because I don't know.'

She grabbed his knees, 'Help me, Father, for Christ's
sake.'

Fidelman, after a short tormented time, said in a quaver-
ing voice, 'I forgive you, my child.'

'The penance,' she wailed, 'first the penance.'

After reflecting, he replied, 'Say one hundred times each,
Our Father and Hail Mary.'

'More,' Annamaria wept. 'More, more. Much more.'

Gripping his knees so hard they shook she burrowed her
head into his black-buttoned lap. He felt the surprised begin-
nings of an erection.

'In that case,' Fidelman said, shuddering a little, 'better
undress.'

'Only,' Annamaria said, 'if you keep your vestments on.'

'Not the cassock, too clumsy.'

'At least the biretta.'

He agreed to that.

Annamaria undressed in a swoop. Her body was extra-
ordinarily lovely, the flesh glowing. In her bed they tightly
embraced. She clasped his buttocks, he cupped hers. Pump-
ing slowly he nailed her to her cross.

paint something. By Jesus, if I could paint myself, that'd show them! Astonished by the thought he ran out of the house.

The art student hastened to a costume shop and settled on a cassock and fuzzy black soupbowl biretta, envisaging another Rembrandt: 'Portrait of the Artist as Priest.' He hurried with his bulky package back to the house. Annamaria was handing the garbage to the portinaia as Fidelman thrust his way into the studio. He quickly changed into the priest's vestments. The pittrice came in wildly to tell him where he got off, but when she saw Fidelman already painting himself as priest, with a moan she rushed into her room. He worked with smoking intensity and in no time created an amazing likeness. Annamaria, after stealthily re-entering the studio, with heaving bosom and agitated eyes closely followed his progress. At last, with a cry she threw herself at his feet.

'Forgive me, Father, for I have sinned –'

Dripping brush in hand, he stared down at her. 'Please, I –'

'Oh, Father, if you knew how I have sinned. I've been a whore –'

After a moment's thought, Fidelman said, 'If so, I absolve you.'

'Not without penance. First listen to the rest. I've had no luck with men. They're all bastards. Or else I jinx them. If you want the truth I am an Evil Eye myself. Anybody who loves me is cursed.'

He listened, fascinated.

'Augusto is really my uncle. After many others he became my lover. At least he's gentle. My father found out and swore he'd kill us both. When I got pregnant I was scared to death. A sin can go too far. Augusto told me to have the baby and leave it at an orphanage, but the night it was

The Death Of Me

Marcus was a tailor, long ago before the war, a buoyant man with a bushy head of greying hair, fine fragile brows and benevolent hands, who comparatively late in life had become a clothier. Because he had prospered, so to say, into ill health, he had to employ an assistant tailor in the rear room, who made alterations on garments but could not, when the work piled high, handle the pressing, so that it became necessary to put on a presser; therefore though the store did well, it did not do too well.

It might have done better but the presser, Josip Bruzak, a heavy, beery, perspiring Pole, who worked in undershirt and felt slippers, his pants loose on his beefy hips, the legs crumpling around his ankles, conceived a violent dislike for Emilio Vizo, the tailor – or it worked the other way, Marcus wasn't sure – a thin, dry, pigeon-chested Sicilian, who bore, or returned the Pole a steely malice. Because of their quarrels the business suffered.

Why they should fight as they did, fluttering and snarling like angry cocks, and using, in the bargain, terrible language, loud coarse words that affronted the customers and sometimes made the embarrassed Marcus feel dizzy to the point of fainting, mystified the clothier, who knew their troubles and felt they were, as people, much alike. Bruzak, who lived in a half-ruined rooming house near the East River, constantly guzzled beer at work and kept a dozen bottles in a rusty pan packed full of ice. When Marcus, in the beginning, objected, Josip, always respectful to the clothier, locked away the pan and disappeared through the

57

back door into the tavern down the block where he had his glass, in the process wasting so much precious time it paid Marcus to advise him to go back to the pan. Every day at lunch Josip pulled out of the drawer a small sharp knife and cut chunks of the hard garlic salami he ate with puffy lumps of white bread, washing it down with beer and then black coffee brewed on the one-burner gas stove for the tailor's iron. Sometimes he cooked up a soupy mess of cabbage which stank up the store, but on the whole neither the salami nor the cabbage interested him, and for days he seemed weary and uneasy until the mailman brought him, about every third week, a letter from the other side. When the letters came, he more than once tore them in half with his bumbling fingers; he forgot his work, and sitting on a backless chair, fished out of the same drawer where he kept his salami, a pair of cracked eye glasses which he attached to his ears by means of looped cords he had tied on in place of the broken side-pieces. Then he read the tissue sheets he held in his fist, a crabbed Polish writing in faded brown ink whose every word he uttered aloud so that Marcus, who understood the language but preferred not to hear, heard. Before the presser had dipped two sentences into the letter, his face dissolved and he cried, oily tears smearing his cheeks and chin so that it looked as though he had been sprayed with something to kill flies. At the end he fell into a roar of sobbing, a terrible thing to behold, which incapacitated him for hours and wasted the morning.

Marcus had often thought of telling him to read his letters at home but the news in them wrung his heart and he could not bring himself to scold Josip, who was, by the way, a master presser. Once he began on a pile of suits, the steaming machine hissed without let-up, and every garment came out neat, without puff or excessive crease, and the arms, legs, and pleats were as sharp as knives. As for the news in the letters it was always the same, concerning the sad experiences of his tubercular wife and unfortunate fourteen-year-old son, whom Josip, except in pictures, had never seen, a boy who lived, literally in the mud with the pigs, and was also sick, so that even if his father saved up money for his passage to America, and the boy could obtain a visa, he would never get past the immigration doctors. Marcus more than once gave the presser a suit of clothes to send to his son, and occasionally some cash, but he wondered if these things ever got to him. He had the uncomfortable thought that Josip, in the last fourteen years, might have brought the boy over had he wanted, his wife too, before she had contracted tuberculosis, but for some reason he preferred to weep over them where they were.

Emilio, the tailor, was another lone wolf. Every day he had a forty-cent lunch in the diner about three blocks away but was always back early to read his *Corriere*. His strangeness was that he was always whispering to himself. No one could understand what he said, but it was sibilant and insistent, and, wherever he was, one could hear his hissing voice urging something, or moaning softly though he never wept. He whispered when he sewed a button on, or shortened a sleeve, or when he used the iron. Whispering when he hung up his coat in the morning, he was still whispering when he put on his black hat, wriggled his sparse shoulders into his coat and left, in loneliness, the store at night. Only once did he hint what the whispering was about; when the clothier, noticing his pallor one morning, brought him a cup of coffee, in gratitude the tailor confided that his wife, who had returned last week, had left him again this, and he held up the outstretched fingers of one bony hand to show she had five times run out on him. Marcus offered the man his sympathy, and thereafter when he heard the tailor whispering in the rear of the store, could always picture the wife

59

coming back to him from wherever she had been, saying she was this time – she swore – going to stay for good, but at night when they were in bed and he was whispering about her in the dark, she would think to herself she could never stand this thing and in the morning, was gone. And so the man's ceaseless whisper irritated Marcus; he had to leave the store to hear silence, yet he kept Emilio on because he was a fine tailor, a demon with a needle, who could sew up a perfect cuff in less time than it takes an ordinary workman to make measurements, the kind of tailor who, when you were looking for one, was very rare.

For more than a year, despite the fact that they both made strange noises in the rear room, neither the presser nor the tailor seemed to notice one another; then one day, as though an invisible wall between them had fallen, they were at each other's throats. Marcus, it appeared, walked in at the very birth of their venom, when, leaving a customer in the store one afternoon, he went back to get a piece of marking chalk and came on a sight that froze him. There they were in the afternoon sunlight that flooded the rear of the shop, momentarily blinding the clothier so that he had time to think he couldn't possibly be seeing what he saw – the two at opposite corners staring stilly at one another – a live, almost hairy staring of intense hatred. The sneering Pole in one trembling hand squeezed a heavy wooden pressing block, while the livid tailor, his back like a cat's against the wall, held aloft in his rigid fingers a pair of cutter's shears.

'What is it?' Marcus shouted when he had recovered his voice, but neither of them would break the stone silence and remained as when he had discovered them, glaring across the shop at the other, the tailor's lips moving noiselessly, and the presser breathing like a dog in heat, an eeriness about them that Marcus had never suspected.

'My God,' he cried, his body drenched in cold creeping

wetness, 'tell me what happened here.' But neither uttered a sound so he shrieked through the constriction in his throat, which made the words grate awfully, 'Go back to work –' hardly believing they would obey; and when they did, Bruzak turning like a lump back to the machine, and the tailor stiffly to his hot iron, Marcus was softened by their compliance and speaking as if to children, said with tears in his eyes, 'Boys, remember, don't fight.'

Afterwards the clothier stood alone in the shade of the store, staring through the glass of the front door at nothing at all; lost, in thinking of them at his very back, in a horrid world of grey grass and green sunlight, of moaning and blood-smell. They had made him dizzy. He lowered himself into the leather chair, praying no customer would enter until he had sufficiently recovered from his nausea. So sighing, he shut his eyes and felt his skull liven with new terror to spy them both engaged in round pursuit in his mind. One ran hot after the other, lumbering but in flight, who had stolen his box of broken buttons. Skirting the lit and smoking sands, they scrambled high up a craggy cliff, locked in many-handed struggle, teetering on the ledge, till one slipped in slime and pulled the other with him. Reaching forth four hands, they clutched nothing in stiffened fingers, as Marcus, the watcher, shrieked without sound at their evanescence.

He sat dizzily until these thoughts had left him.

When he was again himself, remembrance made it a kind of dream. He denied any untoward incident had happened; yet knowing it had, called it a triviality – hadn't he, in the factory he had worked in on coming to America, often seen such fights among the men? – trivial things they all forgot, no matter how momentarily fierce.

However, on the very next day and thereafter daily without skipping a day, the two in the back broke out of their silent hatred into thunderous quarrelling that did damage to the business: in ugly voices they called each other dirty names, embarrassing the clothier so that he threw the measuring tape he wore like a garment on his shoulders, once around the neck. Customer and clothier glanced nervously at each other, and Marcus quickly ran through the measurements; the customer, who as a rule liked to linger in talk of his new clothes, left hurriedly after paying cash, to escape the drone of disgusting names hurled about in the back yet clearly heard in front so that no one had privacy.

Not only would they curse and heap destruction on each other but they muttered in their respective tongues other dreadful things. The clothier understood Josip shouting he would tear off someone's genitals and rub the bloody mess in salt; so he guessed Emilio was shrieking the same things, and was saddened and maddened at once.

He went many times to the rear, pleading with them, and they listened to his every word with interest and tolerance, because the clothier, besides being a kind man – this showed in his eyes – was also eloquent, which they both enjoyed. Yet, whatever his words, they did no good, for the minute he had finished and turned his back on them they began again. Embittered, Marcus withdrew into the store and sat nursing his misery under the yellow-faced clock clicking away yellow minutes, till it was time to stop – it was amazing they got anything done and their work was prodigious – and go home.

His urge was to bounce them out on their behinds but he couldn't conceive where to find two others who were such skilled and, in essence, proficient workers, without having to pay a fortune in gold. Therefore, with reform uppermost in his mind, he caught Emilio one noon as he was leaving for lunch, whispered him into a corner and said, 'Listen, Emilio, you're the smart one, tell me why do you fight?

Why do you hate him and why does he hate you and why do you use such bad words?'

Though he enjoyed the whispering and was soft in the clothier's palms, the tailor, who liked these little attentions, lowered his eyes and blushed darkly but either would not or could not reply.

So Marcus sat under the clock all afternoon with his fingers in his ears. And he caught the presser on his way out that evening and said to him, 'Please, Josip, tell me what he did to you? Josip, why do you fight, you have a sick wife and boy?' But Josip, who also felt an affection for the clothier – he was, despite being Polish, no anti-Semite – merely caught him in his hammy arms, and though he had to clutch at his trousers which were falling and impeding his movements, hugged Marcus into a ponderous polka, then with a cackle, pushed him aside, and in his beer jag, danced away.

When they began the same dirty hullabaloo the next morning and drove a customer out at once, the clothier stormed into the rear and they turned from their cursing – both fatigued and green-grey to the gills – and listened to Marcus begging, shaming, weeping, but especially paid heed when he, who found screeching unsuited to him, dropped it and gave advice and little preachments in a low becoming tone. He was a tall man, and because of his illness, quite thin. What flesh remained had wasted further in these troublesome months, and his hair was white now so that, as he stood before them, expostulating, exhorting, he was in appearance like an old hermit, if not a saint, and the workers showed respect and keen interest as he spoke.

It was a homily about his long-dead dear father, when they were all children living in a rutted village of small huts, a gaunt family of ten – nine boys and an undersized girl. Oh, they were marvellously poor: on occasion he had chewed bark and even grass, bloating his belly, and often the boys bit one another, including the sister, upon the arms and neck in rage at their hunger.

'So my poor father, who had a long beard down to here' – he stooped, reaching his hand to his knee and at once tears sprang up in Josip's eyes – 'my father said, "Children, we are poor people and strangers wherever we go, let us at least live in peace, or if not –"'

But the clothier was not able to finish because the presser, plumped on the backless chair, where he read his letters, swaying a little had begun to whimper and then bawl, and the tailor, who was making odd clicking noises in his throat, had to turn away.

'Promise,' Marcus begged, 'that you won't fight any more.'

Josip wept his promise, and Emilio, with wet eyes, gravely nodded.

This, the clothier exulted, was fellowship, and with a blessing on both their heads, departed, but even before he was altogether gone, the air behind him was greased with their fury.

Twenty-four hours later he fenced them in. A carpenter came and built a thick partition, halving the presser's and tailor's work space, and for once there was astonished quiet between them. They were, in fact, absolutely silent for a full week. Marcus, had he had the energy, would have jumped in joy and kicked his heels together. He noticed, of course, that the presser occasionally stopped pressing and came befuddled to the new door to see if the tailor was still there, and though the tailor did the same, it went no further than that. Thereafter Emilio Vizo no longer whispered to himself and Josip Bruzak touched no beer; and when the emaciated letters arrived from the other side, he took them home to read by the dirty window of his dark room; when night came, though there was electricity, he preferred to read by candlelight.

One Monday morning he opened his table drawer to get at his garlic salami and found it had been roughly broken in two. With his pointed knife raised, he rushed at the tailor, who, at that very moment, because someone had battered his black hat, was coming at him with his burning iron. He caught the presser along the calf of the arm and opened a smelly purple wound, just as Josip stuck him in the groin, and the knife hung there for a minute.

Roaring, wailing, the clothier ran in, and, despite their wounds, sent them packing. When he had left, they locked themselves together and choked necks.

Marcus rushed in again, shouting, 'No, no, please, *please*,' flailing his withered arms, nauseated, enervated (all he could hear in the uproar was the thundering clock), and his heart, like a fragile pitcher, toppled from the shelf and bump bumped down the stairs, cracking at the bottom, the shards flying everywhere.

Although the old Jew's eyes were glazed as he crumpled, the assassins could plainly read in them, What did I tell you? *You see?*

A Choice Of Profession

Cronin, after discovering that his wife, Marge, had been two-timing him with a friend, suffered months of crisis. He had loved Marge and jealousy lingered unbearably. He lived through an anguish of degrading emotions, and a few months after his divorce, left a well-paying job in Chicago to take up teaching. He had always wanted to teach. Cronin taught composition and survey of literature in a small college town in Northern California, and after an initially exhilarating period, began to find it a bore. This caused him worry because he hoped to be at peace in the profession. He wasn't sure whether it was true boredom or simply not knowing whether he wanted to teach the rest of his life. He was bored mostly outside the classroom – the endless grading of papers and book-keeping chores; and for a man of his type, Cronin felt, he had too much to read. He also felt he had been asking from teaching more than he was entitled to. He had always thought of teaching as something religious and perhaps still did. It had to do with giving oneself to others, a way of being he hadn't achieved in his marriage. Cronin, a tall, bulky-shouldered man with sensitive eyes, and a full brown moustache, smoked too much. His trousers were usually smeared with cigarette ashes he brushed off his thighs; and lately, after a period of forbearance, he had begun to drink. Apart from students there were few women around who weren't married, and he was alone too often. Though at the beginning he was invited to faculty parties, he wanted nothing to do with the wives of his colleagues.

The fall wore away. Cronin remained aimlessly in town during the winter vacation. In the spring term a new student, an older girl, appeared in his literature class. Unlike most of the other girls, she wore bright attractive dresses and high heels. She wore her light hair in a bun from which strands slipped but she was otherwise feminine and neat, a mature woman, he realized. Although she wasn't really pretty, her face was open and attractive. Cronin wondered at her experienced eyes and deep-breasted figure. She had slender shoulders and fairly heavy but shapely legs. He thought at first she might be a faculty wife but she was without their combination of articulateness and timidity; he didn't think she was married. He also liked the way she listened to him in class. Many of the students, when he lectured or read poetry, looked sleepy, stupefied, or exalted, but she listened down to bedrock, as if she were expecting a message or had got it. Cronin noticed that the others in the class might listen to the poetry but she listened to Cronin. Her name, not very charming, was Mary Lou Miller. He could tell she regarded him as a man, and after so long a dry, almost perilous season, he responded to her as a woman. Though Cronin wasn't planning to become involved with a student, he had at times considered taking up with this one but resisted it on principle. He wanted to be protected in love by certain rules, but loving a student meant no rules to begin with.

He continued to be interested in her and she occasionally would wait at his desk after class and walk with him in the direction of his office. He often thought she had something personal to say to him, but when she spoke it was usually to say that one or another poem had moved her; her taste, he thought, was a little too inclusive. Mary Lou rarely recited in class. He found her a bit boring when they talked for more than five minutes, but that secretly pleased him because the attraction to her was quite strong and this was a form of insurance. One morning, during a free hour, he went to the registrar's office on some pretext or other, and looked up her records. Cronin was surprised to discover she was twenty-four and only a first-year student. He, though he sometimes felt forty, was twenty-nine. Because they were so close in age, as well as for other reasons, he decided to ask her out. That same afternoon Mary Lou knocked on his office door and came in to see him about a quiz he had just returned. She had got a low C and it worried her. Cronin lit her cigarette and noticed that she watched him intently, his eyes, moustache, hands, as he explained what she might have written on her paper. They were sitting within a foot of one another, and when she raised both arms to fix her bun, the imprint of her large nipples on her dress caught his attention. It was during this talk in the office that he suggested they go for a drive one evening at the end of the week. Mary Lou agreed, saying maybe they could stop off somewhere for a drink, and Cronin, momentarily hesitating, said he thought they might. All the while they had been talking she was looking at him from some inner place in herself, and he had the feeling he had been appraising her superficially.

On the ride that night Mary Lou sat close to Cronin. She had at first sat at the door but soon her warm side was pressed to his though he had not seen her move. They had started at sunset and for an hour the sky was light. The Northern California winter, though colder than he had anticipated, was mild compared to a winter in Chicago, but Cronin was glad to be in touch with spring. He liked the lengthening days, and tonight it was a relief to be with a woman once more. The car passed through a number of neon-lit mountain towns neither of them had been in before, and Cronin noticed that every motel flashed vacancy signs. Part of his good mood was an awareness of the approach of a new season, and part, that he had thought it over and decided there was nothing to worry about. She was a woman, no eighteen-year-old kid he would be taking advantage of. Nor was he married and about to commit adultery. He felt a sincere interest in her.

It was a pleasant evening drive in early March and on their way back they stopped off at a bar in Red Bluff, about forty miles from the college, where it was unlikely anyone they knew would see them. The waiter brought drinks and when Mary Lou had finished hers she excused herself, went to the ladies' room, and upon returning, asked for another on the rocks. She had on a bright blue dress, rather short, and wore no stockings. During the week she used no lip rouge or nail polish; tonight she had both on and Cronin thought he liked her better without them. She smiled at him, her face, after she had had two, flushed. In repose her smile settled into the tail end of bitterness, an expression touched with cynicism, and he wondered about her. They had talked about themselves on the ride, she less than he, Cronin reticently. She had been brought up on a farm in Idaho. He had spent most of his life in Evanston, Illinois, where his grandfather, an evangelical minister, had lived and preached. Cronin's father had died when Cronin was fourteen. Mary Lou told him she had once been married and was now divorced. He had guessed something of the sort and at that point admitted he had been divorced himself. He could feel his leg touching hers under the table and realized it was her doing. Cronin, pretty much contented, had had one drink to her two, and he was nursing his first when she asked for a third. She had become quiet but when their eyes met she smiled again.

'Do you mind if I call you Mary Louise?' Cronin asked her.

'You can if you want to,' she said, 'but my real name is Mary Lou. That's on my birth certificate.'

He asked her how long she had been married before her divorce.

'Oh, just about three years. One that I didn't live with him. How about yourself?'

'Two,' said Cronin.

She drank from her glass. He liked the fact that she was satisfied with a few biographical details. A fuller exchange of information could come later.

He lit a cigarette, only his second since they had come in, whereas she squashed one butt to light another. He wondered why she was nervous.

'Happy?' Cronin asked.

'I'm okay, thanks.' She crushed a newly lit cigarette, thought about it and lit another.

She seemed about to say something, paused, and said, 'How long have you been teaching, if you don't mind me asking you?'

Cronin wondered what was on her mind. 'Not so long,' he answered. 'This is only my first year.'

'You sure put a lot in it.'

He could feel the calf of her leg pressed warmly against his; yet she was momentarily inattentive, vaguely looking around at the people in the bar.

'How about you?' he asked.

'In what ways?'

'How is it you started college so comparatively late?'

She finished her drink. 'I never wanted to go when I graduated high school. Instead I worked a couple of years, then I joined the Wacs.' She fell silent.

He asked if she wanted him to order another drink.

'Not right away.' Mary Lou's eyes focused on his face.

'First I want to tell you something about myself. Do you want to hear it?'

'Yes, if you want to tell me.'

'It's about my life,' Mary Lou said. 'When I was in the Wacs I met this guy, Ray A. Miller, a T-5 from Providence, Rhode Island, and we got hitched in secret in Las Vegas. He was a first-class prick.'

Cronin gazed at her, wondering if she had had one too many. He considered suggesting they leave now but Mary Lou, sitting there solidly, smoking the last cigarette in her pack, told Cronin what she had started out to.

'I call him that word because that's what he was. He married me just to live easy off me. He talked me into doing what he wanted, and I was too goddamn stupid to say no, because at that time I loved him. After we left the service he set me up in this flea-bitten three-room apartment in San Francisco, where I was a call girl. He took the dough and I got the shit.'

'Call girl?' Cronin almost groaned.

'A whore, if you want me to say it.'

Cronin was overwhelmed. He felt a momentary constricting fright and a strange uneasy jealousy, followed by a sense of disappointment and unexpected loss.

'I'm sorry,' he said. Her leg was tense against his but he let his stay though it seemed to him it trembled. His cigarette ash broke, and while brushing it off his thigh, Cronin managed to withdraw his leg from hers. Her face was impassive.

Mary Lou slowly fixed her bun, removing a large number of hairpins and placing them thickly back again.

'I suppose you have a bad opinion of me now?' she said to Cronin, after she had fixed her hair.

71

He said he had no opinion at all, though he knew he had. 'I'm just sorry it happened.'

She looked at him intently. 'One thing I want you to know is I don't have that kind of a life any more. I'm not interested in it. I'm interested in taking it as it comes or goes but not for money any more. That won't happen to me again.'

Cronin said he was surprised it ever had.

'It was just a job I had to do,' Mary Lou explained. 'That's how I thought about it. I kept on it because I was afraid Ray would walk out on me. He always knew what he wanted but I didn't. He was a strong type and I wasn't.'

'Did he walk out?'

She nodded. 'We were having fights about what to do with the dough. He said he was going to start some kind of a business but he never did.'

'That's when you quit?'

She lowered her eyes. 'Not all at once. I stayed for a while to get some money to go to college with. I didn't stay long and I haven't got enough, so I have to work in the cafeteria.'

'When did you finally quit?'

'In three months, when I got arrested.'

He asked about that.

'My apartment was raided by two San Francisco bulls. But it was my first offence so the judge paroled me. I'm paroled now and for one more year.'

'I guess you've been through the mill,' Cronin said, toying with his glass.

'I sure have,' said Mary Lou, 'but I'm not the same person I once was, I learned a lot.'

'Would you care for a last drink before we leave?' he asked. 'It's getting late. We've got an hour's drive.'

'No, but thanks anyway.'

'I'll just have a last drink.'

The waiter brought Cronin a scotch.

'Tell me why you told me this,' he asked Mary Lou after he had drunk from his glass.

'I don't know for sure,' she said. 'Some of it is because I like you. I like the way you teach in your class. That's why I got the idea of telling you.'

'But why, specifically?'

'Because everything's different now.'

'The past doesn't bother you?'

'Not much. I wanted to tell you before this but I couldn't do it in your office without a drink to start me off.'

'Do you want me to do anything for you?' Cronin asked her.

'For instance, what?' said Mary Lou.

'If you want to talk to anybody about yourself I could get you the name of a psychiatrist.'

'Thanks,' she said. 'I don't need one. The guy I talk to about myself will have to do it for nothing, for kicks.'

She asked Cronin for one of his cigarettes and smoked while he finished his drink.

As they were getting ready to leave, Mary Lou said, 'The way I figure, it wasn't all my fault but it's dead and gone now. I got the right to think of the future.'

'You have,' said Cronin.

On the ride home he felt more objective and not unsympathetic to the girl, yet he was still disappointed, and from time to time, irritated with himself.

'Anyway,' Cronin told her, 'you can work for a better way of life now.'

'That's why I want an education for,' Mary Lou said.

2

It took Cronin a surprisingly long time to get over having been let down by Mary Lou. He had built her up in his mind as a woman he might want to spend some time with, and the surprise of her revelation, and his disillusionment, lingered so long he felt unsettled. 'What's this, Marge all over again?' He didn't want any more of that, and not from this girl. He saw her in class, as usual, three times a week. She seemed to listen with the same interest, maybe less interested, but she didn't approach him and no longer waited at his desk to walk with him to his office. Cronin understood that to mean he was to make the next move now that he knew, but he didn't make it. What could he say to her – that he wished he didn't know? Or now that he knew, sometimes when he glanced at her in class he pictured her being paid off by the last guy she had slept with. She was in his thoughts much of the time. He wondered what would have happened that night they were out if she hadn't made that confession. Could he have guessed from the way she performed in bed that she had been a professional? He continued to think of having her and sometimes the thought was so wearing he avoided looking at her in class. He found his desire hard to bear but after a month it wore down. She seemed not very interesting to him then, and he was often aware how hard her expression was. He felt sorry for her and occasionally smiled, and once in a while she seemed cynically to smile back.

Cronin had made friends with a painter, George Getz, an assistant professor in the art department, an active, prematurely bald man, with whom he went on sketching trips, usually on Saturday or Sunday afternoon. George sketched or did water-colours as Cronin looked on or sat against a tree, smoking. Sometimes he wandered along streams and in the woods. When the painter, married from youth and father of three girls, was tied down during the week-end, Cronin drove off by himself or tried walking alone, though generally he cared little for walking in town, and wasn't sure which direction to go next. One fine Sunday in April, when George was busy with his family, Cronin started on a walk but it soon began to seem like work so he returned to his apartment and sat on the bed. Wanting company he searched in his mind for who, and after some doubts looked up Mary Lou Miller's number and dialled it. He wasn't sure why he had, though he knew it bothered him a little. 'Hello there,' she said. She had hesitated on hearing his voice but seemed cordial enough. Cronin wondered about a drive and she said she wouldn't mind. He called for her in his car. She looked a little distant when she came out and he was surprised at how attractive. He noticed she seemed to be prettier on warm days.

'How are things with you?' Cronin asked as he held the door open for her.

'All right, I guess. How are they with you?'

'Fine,' Cronin said.

'How's the teaching?'

'Fine. I'm enjoying it more than I was.'

Not much more but it was too much trouble to explain why.

She seemed at ease. They drove towards the mountains along some of the side roads he had explored with George, until they came to a long blue lake shaped like a bird in flight. Cronin parked the car and they went through a scattering of pine trees, down to the water. At his suggestion they walked part of the way around the lake, and back. It took more than an hour and Mary Lou said she hadn't walked that much in years.

'Life's pleasures are cheap,' Cronin said.

'No, they're not,' said Mary Lou.

He let it pass. They had said nothing about last time, there was nothing to say really. The beauty of the day had lightened Cronin's mood – he remembered having dreamed of Marge last night and had awakened uneasy. But Mary Lou's company, he admitted to himself, had made the walk around the lake enjoyable. She was wearing a yellow cotton dress that showed her figure off, and her hair, to the large thick knot on her neck, was for once neatly arranged. She was rather quiet, as though a word too much might defeat her, but once she loosened up they talked amiably. She seemed to Cronin, as he sat by her side gazing at the lake, no more nor less than any woman he had known. The way he presently saw it was that she was entitled to her mistakes. He was to his. Yet though he tried to forget what she had told him, the fact that she had been a whore kept nagging him. She had known many men, how large a crowd they would make following her now, he was afraid to guess. He had never known anyone like her, and that he was with her now struck him as somewhat strange. But Cronin thought what an unusual thing present time was. In the present a person is what she is becoming and not what she was. She was this heavy-but-shapely-legged girl in a yellow dress, sitting by his side as though she belonged there. Cronin thought this was an interesting lesson for him. The past interfered if you let it. People feared it because they thought it predicted the future. It didn't if you realized how much life changed, and concentrated on what it had changed to, and lived that. He began again to think of the possibility of friendship with Mary Lou.

She got up, brushing pine needles off her dress. 'It's hot,' she said. 'Would you mind if I peeled and went in for a dip?'

'Go ahead,' said Cronin.

'Why don't you come in yourself?' she asked. 'You could keep your shorts on and later get dry in the sun.'

'No, I don't think so,' he said, 'I'm not much of a swimmer.'

'Neither am I,' Mary Lou said, 'but I like the water.'

She unzipped her dress and pulled it over her head. Then she kicked off her shoes, stepped out of a half slip and removed her white underwear. He enjoyed the fullness of her form, the beauty of her breasts. Mary Lou walked into the water, shivered, and began to swim. Cronin sat watching her, one arm around his knees as he smoked. After swimming a while, Mary Lou, her flesh lit in the sunlight, came out of the water, drew on her underpants, then let the sun dry her as she redid her damp hair. He was moved by her wet body after bathing.

When she had dressed, Cronin suggested they have dinner together and Mary Lou agreed. 'But first you come up to my joint for a drink. I want to show you how I fixed it up.'

He said he would like to.

On their ride back she was talkative. She told Cronin about her life as a child. Her father had been a small wheat farmer in Idaho. She had one married sister and two married brothers. She said the oldest brother was a big bastard.

'He's pretty rich by now,' she said, 'and he talks a lot about God's grace but in his heart he is a bastard. When I was thirteen one day he grabbed me in the barn and laid me though I didn't want to.'

'Oh, Christ,' said Cronin. 'You committed incest?'

'It all happened when I was a kid.'

'Why don't you keep these things to yourself?' Cronin said. 'What makes you think I want to hear them?'

'I guess I felt I trusted you.'

'Well, don't trust me,' he shouted.

He drove to her house and let her off at the kerb. Then he drove away.

The next morning Mary Lou did not appear in Cronin's class, and a few days later her drop-slip came through.

3

A week had gone by when Cronin one day saw her walking with George Getz, and his heart was flooded with jealous misery. He thought he was rid of his desire for the girl; but seeing her walking at the painter's side, talking animatedly, George interested, Mary Lou good to look at in a white summer dress and doing very well, thanks, without Cronin, awoke in him a sense of loss and jealousy. He thought he might be in love with her. Cronin watched them go up the stairs of the art building, and though he had no good reason to, pictured them in each other's arms, naked on George's studio couch. The effect was frightening.

My God, thought Cronin, here I am thinking of her with the same miserable feelings I had about Marge. I can't go through that again.

He fought to put her out of his mind – the insistent suspicion of an affair between her and the painter – but his memory of her body at the lake, and imagining the experience she had had with men, what she would do with George, for instance, and might have done with Cronin if they had become lovers, made things worse. Thinking of her experiences was like trying to stop the pain of a particular wound by stabbing yourself elsewhere. His only relief was to get drunk but when that wore off the anguish was worse.

One morning he was so desperately jealous – the most use-less of emotions, and especially useless in a situation where the girl really meant little to him, almost nothing, and the past, despite all his theorizing and good intentions, much too much – that he waited for them for hours, in the foyer of the school of architecture across the street from the art building. Cronin did not at first know why he was waiting but that he had to, perhaps to satisfy himself they were or weren't hav-ing an affair. He saw neither of them then, but on the next afternoon he followed the painter at a distance to Mary Lou's apartment. Cronin saw him go in shortly before five p.m., and was still unhappily waiting under a tree across the street, several houses down, when George came out at half-past ten. Cronin was wakeful all night.

Terrified that this should mean so much to him, he tried to work out some means of relief. Should he telephone the girl and ask her back into his class so that they could once more be on good terms ? Or if that meant trouble with the regis-trar's office, couldn't he just call and apologize for acting as he had, then offer to resume their friendship ? Or could he scare George away by telling him about her past ?

The painter was a family man, a careful sort, and Cronin felt sure he would end it with Mary Lou if he thought any-one suspected he was involved with her ; he wanted to go on feeding his three girls. But telling him about her seemed such a stinking thing to do that Cronin couldn't face it. Still, things were so bad he finally decided to speak to George. He felt that if he could be sure the painter wasn't being intimate with her, his jealousy would die out and the girl fade in his thoughts.

He waited till George invited him on another sketching afternoon, and was glad to have the chance to bring it up then, rather than to have to seek the painter out in his office or studio. They were at the edge of the woods, George at work on a water-colour, when Cronin spoke of the girl and asked whether George knew that Mary Lou had once been a prostitute in San Francisco for a couple of years.

George wiped his brush with a rag, then asked Cronin where he had got his information.

Cronin said he had got it from her. 'She was married to someone who set her up professionally and cut in on the take. After he left her she quit.'

'What a son of a bitch,' said George. He worked for a while, then turned to Cronin and asked, 'Why do you tell me about it?'

'I thought you ought to know.'

'Why ought I?'

'Isn't she a student of yours?'

'No, she isn't. She came to my office and offered to model for me. It's hard to get girls to pose in the nude around here so I said yes. That's all there is between us.'

He seemed embarrassed.

Cronin looked away. 'I didn't think there was anything between you. I just thought you would want to know, if she was your student. I didn't know she wasn't.'

'Well,' said George, 'I know now, but I still intend to use her as a model.'

'I don't see why not.'

'Thanks for telling me, though,' George said. 'I've sometimes felt there's a bit of the slut in her. It wouldn't pay to get involved.'

Cronin, feeling some repulsion for himself, then said, 'To tell the truth, George, I'm not entirely innocent in this. I've wanted to take the girl to bed.'

'Have you?'

'No.'

'I almost did,' George said.

Though Cronin wasn't sure the painter had or hadn't, he was certain he wouldn't dare be intimate with her now. When he got home he felt relief, mingled with shame that had him talking to himself, but he slept better that night.

4

A few nights later Mary Lou rang Cronin's door bell, walked up the stairs, and when she was admitted into his apartment, said she wanted to talk to him. Cronin, reading in pyjamas and robe, offered her a scotch but she refused. Her face was pale, her expression embittered. She was wearing levis and a baggy sweater; the hair spilled out of her bun.

'Look,' Mary Lou said to Cronin, 'I didn't come here for any favours, but did you say anything to Professor Getz about me? I mean what I told you about San Francisco?'

'Did he say I had?' Cronin asked.

'No, but we were being friendly and then he changed to me. I figure somebody must have told him something, and I thought nobody knew anything but you, so you must've told him.'

Cronin admitted it. 'I thought he ought to know, considering the circumstances.'

'Such as what?' she asked sullenly.

He hesitated. 'He's a married man with three kids. There could be serious trouble.'

'That's his goddamn business.'

He admitted that too. 'I'm sorry, Mary Lou. All I can say is that my life has been confused and complicated lately.'

'What about mine?' She was sitting in a chair, then turned her head and wept.

Cronin poured her a drink but Mary Lou wouldn't take it.

'The reason I told you those things is because I thought

you were a guy I could trust and be friends with. Instead it was the opposite. I'm sorry what I told you got you so bothered, but there's a lot worse than that, and one thing I want you to know is it doesn't bother me any more. I made my peace with my life.'

'I haven't,' said Cronin.

'I don't want to hear about it,' said Mary Lou, and though he asked her to stay she left.

Afterwards he thought, She has learned something from her experience that I haven't learned from mine. And he felt sorry for Mary Lou, for the way he had treated her. It's not easy to be moral, Cronin thought. He decided, before he went to bed, not to come back to this college in the fall, to quit teaching.

On Commencement Day, Cronin met Mary Lou in the street, in her yellow dress, and they stopped to talk. She had put on weight but wasn't looking well, and as they talked her stomach rumbled. In embarrassment she covered her abdomen.

'It's from studying,' she said. 'I got awfully worried about my finals. The doctor in the infirmary said to watch out or I might wind up with an ulcer.'

Cronin also advised her to take care. 'Your health comes first.'

They said good-bye. He never saw her again but a year later, in Chicago, he had a card from her. She wrote she was still at college, majoring in education, and hoped some day to teach.

Life Is Better Than Death

She seemed to remember the man from the same day last year. He was standing at a near-by grave, occasionally turning to look around, while Etta, a rosary in her hand, prayed for the repose of the soul of her husband Armando. Sometimes she prayed he would move over and let her lie down with him so that her heart might be eased. It was the second of November, All Souls' Day in the cimitero Campo Verano, in Rome, and it had begun to drizzle after she had laid down the bouquet of yellow chrysanthemums on the grave Armando wouldn't have had if it weren't for a generous uncle, a doctor in Perugia. Without this uncle Etta had no idea where Armando would be buried, certainly in a much less attractive grave, though she would have resisted his often expressed desire to be cremated.

Etta worked for meagre wages in a draper's shop and Armando had left no insurance. The bright large yellow flowers, glowing in November gloom on the faded grass, moved her and tears gushed forth. Although she felt uncomfortably feverish, when she cried like that, Etta was glad she had, because crying seemed to be the only thing that relieved her. She was thirty, dressed in full mourning. Her figure was slim, her moist brown eyes red-rimmed and darkly ringed, the skin pale and her features grown thin. Since the accidental death of Armando, a few months more than a year ago, she came almost daily during the long Roman afternoon rest time to pray at his grave. She was devoted to his memory, ravaged within. Etta went to confession twice a week and took communion every Sunday. She lit candles for Armando

83

at La Madonna Addolorata, and had a mass offered once a month, more often when she had a little extra money. Whenever she returned to the cold inexpensive flat she still lived in and could not give up because it had once also been his, Etta thought of Armando, recalling him as he had looked ten years ago, not as when he had died. Invariably she felt an oppressive pang and ate very little.

It was raining quietly when she finished her rosary. Etta dropped the beads into her purse and opened a black umbrella. The man from the other grave, wearing a darkish green hat and a tight black overcoat, had stopped a few feet behind her, cupping his small hands over a cigarette as he lit it. Seeing her turn from the grave he touched his hat. He was a short man with dark eyes and a barely visible moustache. He had meaty ears but was handsome.

'Your husband?' he asked respectfully, letting the smoke flow out as he spoke, holding his cigarette cupped in his palm to keep it from getting wet.

She was momentarily nervous, undecided whether to do anything more than nod, then go her way, but the thought that he too was bereaved restrained her.

She said it was.

He nodded in the direction of the grave where he had stood. 'My wife. One day while I was on my job she was hurrying to meet a lover and was killed in a minute by a taxi in the Piazza Bologna.' He spoke without bitterness, without apparent emotion, but his eyes were restless.

She noticed that he had put up his coat collar and was getting wet. Hesitantly she offered to share her umbrella with him on the way to the bus stop.

'Cesare Montaldo,' he murmured, gravely accepting the umbrella and holding it high enough for both of them.

'Etta Oliva.' She was, in her high heels, almost a head taller than he.

They walked slowly along an avenue of damp cypresses to the gates of the cemetery, Etta keeping from him that she had been so stricken by his story she could not get out even a sympathetic comment.

'Mourning is a hard business,' Cesare said. 'If people knew there'd be less death.'

She sighed with a slight smile.

Across the street from the bus stop was a 'bar' with tables under a drawn awning. Cesare suggested coffee or perhaps an ice.

She thanked him and was about to refuse but his sad serious expression changed her mind and she went with him across the street. He guided her gently by the elbow, the other hand firmly holding the umbrella over them. She said she felt cold and they went inside.

He ordered an espresso but Etta settled for a piece of pastry which she politely picked at with her fork. Between puffs of a cigarette he talked about himself. His voice was low and he spoke well. He was a free-lance journalist, he said. Formerly he had worked in a government office but the work was boring so he had quit in disgust although he was in line for the directorship. 'I would have directed the boredom.' Now he was toying with the idea of going to America. He had a brother in Boston who wanted him to visit for several months and then decide whether he would emigrate permanently. The brother thought they could arrange that Cesare might come in through Canada. He had considered the idea but could not bring himself to break his ties with this kind of life for that. He seemed also to think that he would find it hard not to be able to go to his dead wife's grave when he was moved to do so. 'You know how it is,' he said, 'with somebody you have once loved.'

Etta felt for her handkerchief in her purse and touched her eyes with it.

'And you?' he asked sympathetically.

To her surprise she began to tell him her story. Though she had often related it to priests, she never had to anyone else, not even a friend. But she was telling it to a stranger because he seemed to be a man who would understand. And if later she regretted telling him, what difference would it make once he had gone?

She confessed she had prayed for her husband's death, and Cesare put down his coffee cup and sat with his butt between his lips, not puffing as she talked.

Armando, Etta said, had fallen in love with a cousin who had come during the summer from Perugia for a job in Rome. Her father had suggested that she live with them, and Armando and Etta, after talking it over, decided to let her stay for a while. They would save her rent to buy a second-hand television set so they could watch 'Lascia o Raddoppia', the quiz programme that everyone in Rome watched on Thursday nights, and that way save themselves the embarrassment of waiting for invitations and having to accept them from neighbours they didn't like. The cousin came, Laura Ansaldo, a big-boned pretty girl of eighteen with thick brown hair and large eyes. She slept on the sofa in the living-room, was easy to get along with, and made herself helpful in the kitchen before and after supper. Etta had liked her until she noticed that Armando had gone mad over the girl. She then tried to get rid of Laura but Armando threatened he would leave if she bothered her. One day Etta had come home from work and found them naked in the marriage bed, engaged in the act. She had screamed and wept. She called Laura a stinking whore and swore she would kill her if she didn't leave the house that minute. Armando was contrite. He promised he would send the girl back to Perugia, and the next day, in the Stazione Termini, had put her on the train. But the separation from her was more than he could bear. He grew nervous and miserable. Armando confessed himself one Saturday night and, for the first time in ten years, took communion, but instead of calming down he desired the girl more strongly. After a week he told Etta that he was going to get his cousin and bring her back to Rome.

'If you bring that whore here,' Etta shouted, 'I'll pray to Christ that you drop dead before you get back.'

'In that case,' Armando said, 'start praying.'

When he left the house she fell on her knees and prayed with all her heart for his death.

That night Armando went with a friend to get Laura. The friend had a truck and was going to Assisi. On the way back he would pick them up in Perugia and drive to Rome. They started out when it was still twilight but it soon grew dark. Armando drove for a while, then felt sleepy and crawled into the back of the truck. The Perugian hills were foggy after a hot September day and the truck hit a rock in the road a hard bump. Armando, in deep sleep, rolled out of the open tailgate of the truck, hitting the road with head and shoulders then rolling down the hill. He was dead before he stopped rolling. When she heard of this Etta fainted away and it was two days before she could speak. After that she had prayed for her own death and often did.

Etta turned her back to the other tables, though they were empty, and wept openly and quietly.

After a while Cesare squashed his butt. 'Calma, Signora. If God had wanted your husband to live he would still be living. Prayers have little relevance to the situation. To my way of thinking the whole thing was no more than a coincidence. It's best not to go too far with religion or it becomes troublesome.'

'A prayer is a prayer,' she said. 'I suffer for mine.'

Cesare pursed his lips. 'But who can judge these things?

They're much more complicated than most of us know. In the case of my wife I didn't pray for her death but I confess I might have wished it. Am I in a better position than you?'

'My prayer was a sin. You don't have that on your mind. It's worse than what you just might have thought.'

'That's only a technical thing, Signora.'

'If Armando had lived,' she said after a minute, 'he would have been twenty-nine next month. I am a year older. But my life is useless now. I want to join him.'

He shook his head, seemed moved, and ordered an espresso for her.

Though Etta had stopped crying, for the first time in months she felt substantially disburdened.

Cesare put her on the bus; as they were crossing the street he suggested they might meet now and then since they had so much in common.

'I live like a nun,' she said.

He lifted his hat. 'Coraggio,' and she smiled at him for his kindness.

When she returned home that night the anguish of life without Armando recommenced. She remembered him as he had been when he was courting her and felt uneasy for having talked about him to Cesare. And she vowed for herself continued prayers, rosaries, her own penitence to win him further indulgences in Purgatory.

Etta saw Cesare on a Sunday afternoon a week later. He had written her name in his little book and was able to locate her apartment in a house on the via Nomentana through the help of a friend in the electric company.

When he knocked on her door she was surprised to see him, turned rather pale, though he hung back doubtfully. But she invited him in and he entered apologetically. He said he had found out by accident where she lived and she asked for no details. Cesare had brought a small bunch of violets which she embarrassedly accepted and put in water.

'You're looking better, Signora,' he said.

'My mourning for Armando goes on,' she answered with a sad smile.

'Moderazione,' he counselled, flicking his meaty ear with his pinky. 'You're still a young woman, and at that not bad looking. You ought to acknowledge it to yourself. There are certain advantages to self belief.'

Etta made coffee and Cesare insisted on going out for a half-dozen pastries.

He said as they were eating that he was considering emigrating if nothing better turned up soon. After a pause he said he had decided he had given more than his share to the dead. 'I've been faithful to her memory but I have to think of myself once in a while. There comes a time when one has to return to life. It's only natural. Where there's life there's life.'

She lowered her eyes and sipped her coffee.

Cesare set down his cup and got up. He put on his coat and thanked her. As he was buttoning his overcoat he said he would drop by again when he was in the neighbourhood. He had a journalist friend who lived close by.

'Don't forget I'm still in mourning,' Etta said.

He looked up at her respectfully. 'Who can forget that, Signora? Who would want to so long as you mourn?'

She then felt uneasy.

'You know my story.' She spoke as though she were explaining again.

'I know,' he said, 'that we were both betrayed. They died and we suffer. My wife ate flowers and I belch.'

'They suffer too. If Armando must suffer, I don't want it to be about me. I want him to feel that I'm still married to him.' Her eyes were wet again.

'He's dead, Signora. The marriage is over,' Cesare said.

89

'There's no marriage without his presence unless you expect the Holy Ghost.' He spoke dryly, adding quietly, 'Your needs are different from a dead man's, you're a healthy woman. Let's face the facts.'

'Not spiritually,' she said quickly.

'Spiritually and physically, there's no love in death.'

She blushed and spoke in excitement. 'There's love for the dead. Let him feel that I'm paying for my sin at the same time he is for his. To help him into heaven I keep myself pure. Let him feel that.'

Cesare nodded and left, but Etta, after he had gone, continued to be troubled. She felt uneasy, could not define her mood, and stayed longer than usual at Armando's grave when she went the next day. She promised herself not to see Cesare again. In the next weeks she became a little miserly.

The journalist returned one evening almost a month later and Etta stood at the door in a way that indicated he would not be asked in. She had seen herself doing this if he appeared. But Cesare, with his hat in his hand, suggested a short stroll. The suggestion seemed so modest that she agreed. They walked down the via Nomentana, Etta wearing her highest heels, Cesare unselfconsciously talking. He wore small patent leather shoes and smoked as they strolled.

It was already early December, still late autumn rather than winter. A few leaves clung to a few trees and a warmish mist hung in the air. For a while Cesare talked of the political situation but after an espresso in a bar on the via Venti Settembre, as they were walking back he brought up the subject she had hoped to avoid. Cesare seemed suddenly to have lost his calm, unable to restrain what he had been planning to say. His voice was intense, his gestures impatient, his dark eyes restless. Although his outburst frightened her she could do nothing to prevent it.

'Signora,' he said, 'wherever your husband is you're not

helping him by putting this penance on yourself. To help him, the best thing you can do is take up your normal life. Otherwise he will continue to suffer doubly, once for something he was guilty of and the second time for the unfair burden your denial of life imposes on him.'

'I am repenting my sins, not punishing him.' She was too disturbed to say more, considered walking home wordless, then slamming the front door in his face; but she heard herself hastily saying, 'If we became intimate it would be like adultery. We would both be betraying the dead.'

'Why is it you see everything in reverse ?'

Cesare had stopped under a tree and almost jumped as he spoke. 'They – *they* betrayed us. If you'll pardon me, Signora, the truth is my wife was a pig. Your husband was a pig. We mourn because we hate them. Let's have the dignity to face the facts.'

'No more,' she moaned, hastily walking on. 'Don't say anything else, I don't want to hear it.'

'Etta,' said Cesare passionately, walking after her, 'this is my last word and then I'll nail my tongue to my jaw. Just remember this. If Our Lord Himself this minute let Armando rise from the dead to take up his life on earth, tonight – he would be lying in his cousin's bed.'

She began to cry, Etta walked on, crying, realizing the truth of his remark. Cesare seemed to have said all he had wanted to, gently held her arm, breathing heavily as he escorted her back to her apartment. At the outer door, as she was trying to think how to get rid of him, how to end this, without waiting a minute he tipped his hat and walked off.

For more than a week Etta went through many torments. She felt a passionate desire to sleep with Cesare. Overnight her body became a torch. Her dreams were erotic. She saw Armando naked in bed with Laura, and in the same bed she saw herself with Cesare, clasping his small body to hers. But she resisted – prayed, confessed her most lustful thoughts, and stayed for hours at Armando's grave to calm her mind.

Cesare knocked at her door one night, and because she was repelled when he suggested the marriage bed, went with him to his rooms. Though she felt guilty afterwards she continued to visit Armando's grave, though less frequently, and she didn't tell Cesare that she had been to the cemetery when she went to his flat afterwards. Nor did he ask her, nor talk about his wife or Armando.

At first her uneasiness was intense. Etta felt as though she had committed adultery against the memory of her husband, but when she told herself over and over – there was no husband, he was dead; there was no husband, she was alone; she began to believe it. There was no husband, there was only his memory. She was not committing adultery. She was a lonely woman and had a lover, a widower, a gentle and affectionate man.

One night as they were lying in bed she asked Cesare about the possibility of marriage and he said that love was more important. They both knew how marriage destroyed love.

And when two months later, she found she was pregnant and hurried that morning to Cesare's rooms to tell him, the journalist, in his pyjamas, calmed her. 'Let's not regret human life.'

'It's your child,' said Etta.

'I'll acknowledge it as mine,' Cesare said, and Etta went home happy.

The next day, when she returned at her usual hour, after having told Armando at his grave that she was at last going to have a baby, Cesare was gone.

'Moved,' the landlady said, with a poof of her hand, and she didn't know where.

Though Etta's heart hurt and she deeply mourned the

loss of Cesare, try as she would she could not, even with the life in her belly, escape thinking of herself as an adulteress, and she never returned to the cemetery to stand again at Armando's grave.

The Jewbird

The window was open so the skinny bird flew in. Flappity-flap with its frazzled black wings. That's how it goes. It's open, you're in. Closed, you're out and that's your fate. The bird wearily flapped through the open kitchen window of Harry Cohen's top-floor apartment on First Avenue near the lower East River. On a rod on the wall hung an escaped canary cage, its door wide open, but this black-type long-beaked bird – its ruffled head and small dull eyes, crossed a little, making it look like a dissipated crow – landed if not smack on Cohen's thick lamb chop, at least on the table, close by. The frozen foods salesman was sitting at supper with his wife and young son on a hot August evening a year ago. Cohen, a heavy man with hairy chest and beefy shorts; Edie, in skinny yellow shorts and red halter; and their ten-year-old Morris (after her father) – Maurie, they called him, a nice kid though not overly bright – were all in the city after two weeks out, because Cohen's mother was dying. They had been enjoying Kingston, New York, but drove back when Mama got sick in her flat in the Bronx.

'Right on the table,' said Cohen, putting down his beer glass and swatting at the bird. 'Son of a bitch.'

'Harry, take care with your language,' Edie said, looking at Maurie, who watched every move.

The bird cawed hoarsely and with a flap of its bedraggled wings – feathers tufted this way and that – rose heavily to the top of the open kitchen door, where it perched staring down.

'Gevalt, a pogrom!'

'Feed him out on the balcony,' Cohen said. He spoke to the bird. 'After that take off.'

Schwartz closed both bird eyes. 'I'm tired and it's a long way.'

'Which direction are you headed, north or south?'

Schwartz, barely lifting his wings, shrugged.

'You don't know where you're going?'

'Where there's charity I'll go.'

'Let him stay, papa,' said Maurie. 'He's only a bird.'

'So stay the night,' Cohen said, 'but no longer.'

In the morning Cohen ordered the bird out of the house but Maurie cried, so Schwartz stayed for a while. Maurie was still on vacation from school and his friends were away. He was lonely and Edie enjoyed the fun he had, playing with the bird.

'He's no trouble at all,' she told Cohen, 'and besides his appetite is very small.'

'What'll you do when he makes dirty?'

'He flies across the street in a tree when he makes dirty, and if nobody passes below, who notices?'

'So all right,' said Cohen, 'but I'm dead set against it. I warn you he ain't gonna stay here long.'

'What have you got against the poor bird?'

'Poor bird, my ass. He's a foxy bastard. He thinks he's a Jew.'

'What difference does it make what he thinks?'

'A Jewbird, what a chuzpah. One false move and he's out on his drumsticks.'

At Cohen's insistence Schwartz lived out on the balcony in a new wooden birdhouse Edie had bought him.

'With many thanks,' said Schwartz, 'though I would rather have a human roof over my head. You know how it is at my age. I like the warm, the windows, the smell of cooking. I would also be glad to see once in a while the

Jewish Morning Journal and have now and then a schnapps because it helps my breathing, thanks God. But whatever you give me, you won't hear complaints.'

However, when Cohen brought home a bird feeder full of dried corn, Schwartz said, 'Impossible.'

Cohen was annoyed. 'What's the matter, crosseyes, is your life getting too good for you? Are you forgetting what it means to be migratory? I'll bet a helluva lot of crows you happen to be acquainted with, Jews or otherwise, would give their eyeteeth to eat this corn.'

Schwartz did not answer. What can you say to a grubber yung?

'Not for my digestion,' he later explained to Edie. 'Cramps. Herring is better even if it makes you thirsty. At least rainwater don't cost anything.' He laughed sadly in breathy caws.

And herring, thanks to Edie, who knew where to shop, was what Schwartz got, with an occasional piece of potato pancake, and even a bit of soupmeat when Cohen wasn't looking.

When school began in September, before Cohen would once again suggest giving the bird the boot, Edie prevailed on him to wait a little while until Maurie adjusted.

'To deprive him right now might hurt his school work, and you know what trouble we had last year.'

'So okay, but sooner or later the bird goes. That I promise you.'

Schwartz, though nobody had asked him, took on full responsibility for Maurie's performance in school. In return for favours granted, when he was let in for an hour or two at night, he spent most of his time overseeing the boy's lessons. He sat on top of the dresser near Maurie's desk as he laboriously wrote out his homework. Maurie was a restless type and Schwartz gently kept him to his studies. He also listened to him practise his screechy violin, taking a few minutes off now and then to rest his ears in the bathroom. And they afterwards played dominoes. The boy was an indifferent checker player and it was impossible to teach him chess. When he was sick, Schwartz read him comic books though he personally disliked them. But Maurie's work improved in school and even his violin teacher admitted his playing was better. Edie gave Schwartz credit for these improvements though the bird pooh-poohed them.

Yet he was proud there was nothing lower than C minuses on Maurie's report card, and on Edie's insistence celebrated with a little schnapps.

'If he keeps up like this,' Cohen said, 'I'll get him in an Ivy League college for sure.'

'Oh I hope so,' sighed Edie.

But Schwartz shook his head. 'He's a good boy – you don't have to worry. He won't be a shicker or a wifebeater, God forbid, but a scholar he'll never be, if you know what I mean, although maybe a good mechanic. It's no disgrace in these times.'

'If I were you,' Cohen said, angered, 'I'd keep my big snoot out of other people's private business.'

'Harry, please,' said Edie.

'My goddamn patience is wearing out. That crosseyes butts into everything.'

Though he wasn't exactly a welcome guest in the house, Schwartz gained a few ounces although he did not improve in appearance. He looked bedraggled as ever, his feathers unkempt, as though he had just flown out of a snowstorm. He spent, he admitted, little time taking care of himself. Too much to think about. 'Also outside plumbing,' he told Edie. Still there was more glow to his eyes so that though

Cohen went on calling him crosseyes he said it less emphatically.

Liking his situation, Schwartz tried tactfully to stay out of Cohen's way, but one night when Edie was at the movies and Maurie was taking a hot shower, the frozen foods salesman began a quarrel with the bird.

'For Christ sake, why don't you wash yourself sometimes? Why must you always stink like a dead fish?'

'Mr Cohen, if you'll pardon me, if somebody eats garlic he will smell from garlic. I eat herring three times a day. Feed me flowers and I will smell like flowers.'

'Who's obligated to feed you anything at all? You're lucky to get herring.'

'Excuse me, I'm not complaining,' said the bird. 'You're complaining.'

'What's more,' said Cohen, 'even from out on the balcony I can hear you snoring away like a pig. It keeps me awake at night.'

'Snoring,' said Schwartz, 'isn't a crime, thanks God.'

'All in all you are a goddamn pest and free loader. Next thing you'll want to sleep in bed next to my wife.'

'Mr Cohen,' said Schwartz, 'on this, rest assured. A bird is a bird.'

'So you say, but how do I know you're a bird and not some kind of a goddamn devil?'

'If I was a devil you would know already. And I don't mean because your son's good marks.'

'Shut up, you bastard bird,' shouted Cohen.

'Grubber yung,' cawed Schwartz, rising to the tips of his talons, his long wings outstretched.

Cohen was about to lunge for the bird's scrawny neck but Maurie came out of the bathroom, and for the rest of the evening until Schwartz's bedtime on the balcony, there was pretended peace.

But the quarrel had deeply disturbed Schwartz and he slept badly. His snoring woke him, and awake, he was fearful of what would become of him. Wanting to stay out of Cohen's way, he kept to the birdhouse as much as possible. Cramped by it, he paced back and forth on the balcony ledge, or sat on the birdhouse roof, staring into space. In the evenings, while overseeing Maurie's lessons, he often fell asleep. Awakening, he nervously hopped around exploring the four corners of the room. He spent much time in Maurie's closet, and carefully examined his bureau drawers when they were left open. And once when he found a large paper bag on the floor, Schwartz poked his way into it to investigate what possibilities were. The boy was amused to see the bird in the paper bag.

'He wants to build a nest,' he said to his mother.

Edie, sensing Schwartz's unhappiness, spoke to him quietly.

'Maybe if you did some of the things my husband wants you, you would get along better with him.'

'Give me a for instance,' Schwartz said.

'Like take a bath, for instance.'

'I'm too old for baths,' said the bird. 'My feathers fall out without baths.'

'He says you have a bad smell.'

'Everybody smells. Some people smell because of their thoughts or because who they are. My bad smell comes from the food I eat. What does his comes from?'

'I better not ask him or it might make him mad,' said Edie.

In late November Schwartz froze on the balcony in the fog and cold, and especially on rainy days he woke with stiff joints and could barely move his wings. Already he felt twinges of rheumatism. He would have liked to spend more time in the warm house, particularly when Maurie was in school and Cohen at work. But though Edie was good-hearted and might have sneaked him in in the morning, just to thaw out, he was afraid to ask her. In the meantime Cohen, who had been reading articles about the migration of birds, came out on the balcony one night after work when Edie was in the kitchen preparing pot roast, and peeking into the birdhouse, warned Schwartz to be on his way soon if he knew what was good for him. 'Time to hit the flyways.'

'Mr Cohen, why do you hate me so much?' asked the bird. 'What did I do to you?'

'Because you're an A-number-one trouble maker, that's why. What's more, whoever heard of a Jewbird? Now scat or it's open war.'

But Schwartz stubbornly refused to depart so Cohen embarked on a campaign of harassing him, meanwhile hiding it from Edie and Maurie. Maurie hated violence and Cohen didn't want to leave a bad impression. He thought maybe if he played dirty tricks on the bird he would fly off without being physically kicked out. The vacation was over, let him make his easy living off the fat of somebody else's land. Cohen worried about the effect of the bird's departure on Maurie's schooling but decided to take the chance, first, because the boy now seemed to have the knack of studying – give the black bird-bastard credit – and second, because Schwartz was driving him bats by being there always, even in his dreams.

The frozen foods salesman began his campaign against the bird by mixing watery cat food with the herring slices in Schwartz's dish. He also blew up and popped numerous paper bags outside the birdhouse as the bird slept, and when he had got Schwartz good and nervous, though not enough to leave, he brought a full-grown cat into the house, supposedly a gift for little Maurie, who had always wanted a pussy. The cat never stopped springing up at Schwartz whenever he saw him, one day managing to claw out several of his tailfeathers. And even at lesson time, when the cat was usually excluded from Maurie's room, though somehow or other he quickly found his way in at the end of the lesson, Schwartz was desperately fearful of his life and flew from pinnacle to pinnacle – light fixture to clothes-tree to door-top – in order to elude the beast's wet jaws.

Once when the bird complained to Edie how hazardous his existence was, she said, 'Be patient, Mr Schwartz. When the cat gets to know you better he won't try to catch you any more.'

'When he stops trying we will both be in Paradise,' Schwartz answered. 'Do me a favour and get rid of him. He makes my whole life worry. I'm losing feathers like a tree loses leaves.'

'I'm awfully sorry but Maurie likes the pussy and sleeps with it.'

What could Schwartz do? He worried but came to no decision, being afraid to leave. So he ate the herring garnished with cat food, tried hard not to hear the paper bags bursting like fire crackers outside the birdhouse at night, and lived terror-stricken closer to the ceiling than the floor, as the cat, his tail flicking, endlessly watched him.

Weeks went by. Then on the day after Cohen's mother had died in her flat in the Bronx, when Maurie came home with a zero on an arithmetic test, Cohen, enraged, waited until Edie had taken the boy to his violin lesson, then openly attacked the bird. He chased him with a broom on the balcony and Schwartz frantically flew back and forth, finally escaping into his birdhouse. Cohen triumphantly reached in, and grabbing both skinny legs, dragged the bird out, cawing loudly, his wings wildly beating. He whirled the bird around and around his head. But Schwartz, as he moved in circles, managed to swoop down and catch Cohen's nose in his beak, and hung on for dear life. Cohen cried out in great pain, punched the bird with his fist, and tugging at its legs with all his might, pulled his nose free. Again he swung the yawking Schwartz around until the bird grew dizzy, then with a furious heave, flung him into the night. Schwartz sank like stone into the street. Cohen then tossed the birdhouse and feeder after him, listening at the ledge until they crashed on the sidewalk below. For a full hour, broom in hand, his heart palpitating and nose throbbing with pain, Cohen waited for Schwartz to return but the broken-hearted bird didn't.

That's the end of that dirty bastard, the salesman thought and went in. Edie and Maurie had come home.

'Look,' said Cohen, pointing to his bloody nose swollen three times its normal size, 'what that sonofabitchy bird did. It's a permanent scar.'

'Where is he now?' Edie asked, frightened.

'I threw him out and he flew away. Good riddance.'

Nobody said no, though Edie touched a handkerchief to her eyes and Maurie rapidly tried the nine-times table and found he knew approximately half.

In the spring when the winter's snow had melted, the boy moved by a memory, wandered in the neighbourhood, looking for Schwartz. He found a dead black bird in a small lot near the river, his two wings broken, neck twisted, and both bird-eyes plucked clean.

'Who did it to you, Mr Schwartz?' Maurie wept.

'Anti-Semeets,' Edie said later.

Naked Nude

Fidelman listlessly doodled all over a sheet of yellow paper. Odd indecipherable designs, ink-spotted blotched words, esoteric ideographs, tormented figures in a steaming sulphurous lake, including a stylish nude rising newborn from the water. Not bad at all, though more mannequin than Knidean Aphrodite. Scarpio, sharp-nosed on the former art student's gaunt left, looking up from his cards inspected her with his good eye.

'Not bad, who is she?'

'Nobody I really know.'

'You must be hard up.'

'It happens in art.'

'Quiet,' rumbled Angelo, the padrone, on Fidelman's fat right, his two-chinned face moulded in lard. He flipped the top card.

Scarpio then turned up a deuce, making eight and a half and out. He cursed his Sainted Mother, Angelo wheezing. Fidelman showed four and his last hundred lire. He picked a cautious ace and sighed. Angelo, with seven showing, chose that passionate moment to get up and relieve himself.

'Wait for me,' he ordered. 'Watch the money, Scarpio.'

'Who's that hanging?' Scarpio pointed to a long-coated figure loosely dangling from a gallows rope amid Fidelman's other drawings.

Who but Susskind, surely, a figure out of the far-off past.

'Just a friend.'

'Which one?'

'Nobody you know.'

'It better not be.'

Scarpio picked up the yellow paper for a closer squint.

'But whose head?' he asked with interest. A long-nosed severed head bounced down the steps of the guillotine platform.

A man's head or his sex? Fidelman wondered. In either case a terrible wound.

'Looks a little like mine,' he confessed. 'At least the long jaw.'

Scarpio pointed to a street scene. In front of American Express here's this starving white Negro pursued by a hooting mob of cowboys on horses.

Embarrassed by the recent past Fidelman blushed.

It was long after midnight. They sat motionless in Angelo's stuffy office, a small lit bulb hanging down over a square wooden table on which lay a pack of puffy cards, Fidelman's naked hundred-lire note, and a green bottle of Munich beer that the padrone of the Hôtel du Ville, Milano, swilled from, between hands or games. Scarpio, his majordomo and secretary-lover, sipped an espresso, and Fidelman only watched, being without privileges. Each night they played sette e mezzo, jeenrummy or baccarat and Fidelman lost the day's earnings, the few meagre tips he had garnered from the whores for little services rendered. Angelo said nothing and took all.

Scarpio, snickering, understood the street scene. Fidelman, adrift penniless in the stony grey Milanese streets, had picked his first pocket, of an American tourist staring into a store window. The Texan, feeling the tug, and missing his wallet, had bellowed murder. A carabiniere looked wildly at Fidelman, who broke into a run, another well-dressed carabiniere on a horse clattering after him down the street, waving his sword. Angelo, cleaning his fingernails with his

penknife in front of his hotel, saw Fidelman coming and
ducked him around a corner, through a cellar door, into the
Hôtel du Ville, a joint for prostitutes who split their fees
with the padrone for the use of a room. Angelo registered
the former art student, gave him a tiny dark room, and,
pointing a gun, relieved him of his passport, recently renewed, and the contents of the Texan's wallet. He warned
him that if he so much as peeped to anybody, he would at
once report him to the questura, where his brother pre-
sided, as a dangerous alien thief. The former art student,
desperate to escape, needed money to travel, so he sneaked
into Angelo's room one morning and from the strapped
suitcase under the bed, extracted fistsful of lire, stuffing all
his pockets. Scarpio, happening in, caught him at it and held
a pointed dagger to Fidelman's ribs – who fruitlessly
pleaded they could both make a living from the suitcase –
until the padrone appeared.

'A hunchback is straight only in the grave.' Angelo slapped Fidelman's face first with one fat hand, then with the
other, till it turned red and the tears freely flowed. He
chained him to the bed in his room for a week. When Fidelman promised to behave he was released and appointed
'mastro delle latrine', having to clean thirty toilets every
day with a stiff brush, for room and board. He also assisted
Teresa, the asthmatic, hairy-legged chambermaid, and ran
errands for the whores. The former art student hoped to
escape but the portiere or his assistant was at the door
twenty-four hours a day. And thanks to the card games and
his impassioned gambling Fidelman was without sufficient
funds to go anywhere, if there was anywhere to go. And
without passport, so he stayed put.

Scarpio secretly felt Fidelman's thigh.

'Let go or I'll tell the padrone.'

Angelo returned and flipped up a card. Queen. Seven and

a half on the button. He pocketed Fidelman's last hundred lire.

'Go to bed,' Angelo commanded. 'It's a long day tomorrow.'

Fidelman climbed up to his room on the fifth floor and stared out the window into the dark street to see how far down was death. Too far, so he undressed for bed. He looked every night and sometimes during the day. Teresa, screaming, had once held on to both his legs as Fidelman dangled half out of the window until one of the girl's naked customers, a barrel-chested man, rushed into the room and dragged him back in. Sometimes Fidelman wept in his sleep.

He awoke, cringing. Angelo and Scarpio had entered his room but nobody hit him.

'Search anywhere,' he offered, 'you won't find anything except maybe half a stale pastry.'

'Shut up,' said Angelo. 'We came to make a proposition.'

Fidelman slowly sat up. Scarpio produced the yellow sheet he had doodled on. 'We notice you draw.' He pointed a dirty fingernail at the nude figure.

'After a fashion,' Fidelman said modestly. 'I doodle and see what happens.'

'Could you copy a painting?'

'What sort of painting?'

'A nude. Tiziano's "Venus of Urbino". The one after Giorgione.'

'That one,' said Fidelman, thinking. 'I doubt that I could.'

'Any fool can.'

'Shut up, Scarpio,' Angelo said. He sat his bulk at the foot of Fidelman's narrow bed. Scarpio, with his good eye, moodily inspected the cheerless view from the window.

'On Isola Bella in Lago Maggiore, about an hour from here,' said Angelo, 'there's a small castello full of lousy paintings, except for one which is a genuine Tiziano, authenticated by three art experts, including a brother-in-law of mine. It's worth half a million dollars but the owner is richer than Olivetti and won't sell though an American museum is breaking its head to get it.'

'Very interesting,' Fidelman said.

'Exactly,' said Angelo. 'Anyway, it's insured for at least $400,000. Of course if anyone stole it it would be impossible to sell.'

'Then why bother?'

'Bother what?'

'Whatever it is,' Fidelman said lamely.

'You'll learn more by listening,' Angelo said. 'Suppose it was stolen and held for ransom. What do you think of that?'

'Ransom?' said Fidelman.

'Ransom,' Scarpio said from the window.

'At least $300,000,' said Angelo. 'It would be a bargain for the insurance company. They'd save a hundred thousand on the deal.'

He outlined a plan. They had photographed the Titian on both sides, from all angles and several distances and had collected from art books the best colour plates. They also had the exact measurements of the canvas and every figure on it. If Fidelman could make a decent copy they would duplicate the frame and on a dark night sneak the reproduction into the castello gallery and exit with the original. The guards were stupid, and the advantage of the plan – instead of just slitting the canvas out of its frame – was that nobody would recognize the substitution for days, possibly longer. In the meantime they would row the picture across the lake and truck it out of the country down to the French Riviera. The

Italian police had fantastic luck in recovering stolen paintings; one had a better chance in France. Once the picture
was securely hidden, Angelo back at the hotel, Scarpio
would get in touch with the insurance company. Imagine
the sensation! Recognizing the brilliance of the execution,
the company would have to kick in with the ransom money.

'If you make a good copy, you'll get yours,' said Angelo.

'Mine? What would that be?' Fidelman asked.

'Your passport,' Angelo said cagily. 'Plus two hundred
dollars in cash and a quick good-bye.'

'Five hundred dollars,' said Fidelman.

'Scarpio,' said the padrone patiently, 'show him what you
have in your pants.'

Scarpio unbuttoned his jacket and drew a long mean-
looking dagger from a sheath under his belt. Fidelman,
without trying, could feel the cold blade sinking into his
ribs.

'Three fifty,' he said. 'I'll need plane fare.'

'Three fifty,' said Angelo. 'Payable when you deliver the
finished reproduction.'

'And you pay for all supplies?'

'I pay all expenses within reason. But if you try any mon-
key tricks – snitch or double cross you'll wake up with your
head gone, or something worse.'

'Tell me,' Fidelman asked after a minute of contempla-
tion, 'what if I turn down the proposition? I mean in a
friendly way?'

Angelo rose sternly from the creaking bed. 'Then you'll
stay here for the rest of your life. When you leave you leave
in a coffin, very cheap wood.'

'I see,' said Fidelman.

'What do you say?'

'What more can I say?'

'Then it's settled,' said Angelo.

'Take the morning off,' said Scarpio.

'Thanks,' Fidelman said.

Angelo glared. 'First finish the toilet bowls.'

Am I worthy? Fidelman thought. Can I do it? Do I dare? He had these and other doubts, felt melancholy, and wasted time.

Angelo one morning called him into his office. 'Have a Munich beer.'

'No, thanks.'

'Cordial?'

'Nothing now.'

'What's the matter with you? You look like you buried your mother.'

Fidelman set down his mop and pail with a sigh and said nothing.

'Why don't you put those things away and get started?' the padrone asked, 'I've had the portiere move six trunks and some broken furniture out of the storeroom where you have two big windows. Scarpio wheeled in an easel and he's bought you brushes, colours and whatever else you need.'

'It's west light, not very even.'

Angelo shrugged. 'It's the best I can do. This is our season and I can't spare any rooms. If you'd rather work at night we can set up some lamps. It's a waste of electricity but I'll make that concession to your temperament if you work fast and produce the goods.'

'What's more I don't know the first thing about forging paintings,' Fidelman said. 'All I might do is just about copy the picture.'

'That's all we ask. Leave the technical business to us. First do a decent drawing. When you're ready to paint I'll get you a piece of sixteenth-century Belgian linen that's been scraped clean of a former picture. You prime it with white lead and when it's dry you sketch. Once you finish the nude, Scarpio and I will bake it, put in the cracks, and age them with soot. We'll even stipple in fly spots before we varnish and glue. We'll do what's necessary. There are books on this subject and Scarpio reads like a demon. It isn't as complicated as you think.'

'What about the truth of the colours?'

'I'll mix them for you. I've made a life study of Tiziano's work.'

'Really?'

'Of course.'

But Fidelman's eyes still looked unhappy.

'What's eating you now?' the padrone asked.

'It's stealing another painter's ideas and work.'

The padrone wheezed. 'Tiziano will forgive you. Didn't he steal the figure of the Urbino from Giorgione? Didn't Rubens steal the Andrian nude from Tiziano? Art steals and so does everybody. You stole a wallet and tried to steal my lire. It's the way of the world. We're only human.'

'Isn't it sort of a desecration?'

'Everybody desecrates. We live off the dead and they live off us. Take for instance religion.'

'I don't think I can do it without seeing the original,' Fidelman said. 'The colour plates you gave me aren't true.'

'Neither is the original any more. You don't think Rembrandt painted in those sfumato browns? As for painting the Venus, you'll have to do the job here. If you copied it in the castello gallery one of those cretin guards might remember your face and the next thing you know you'd have trouble. So would we, probably, and we naturally wouldn't want that.'

'I still ought to see it,' Fidelman said obstinately.

The padrone then reluctantly consented to a one-day excursion to Isola Bella, assigning Scarpio to closely accompany the copyist.

On the vaporetto to the island, Scarpio, wearing dark glasses and a light straw hat, turned to Fidelman.

'In all confidence, what do you think of Angelo?'

'He's all right, I guess.'

'Do you think he's handsome?'

'I haven't given it a thought. Possibly he was, once.'

'You have many fine insights,' said Scarpio. He pointed in the distance where the long blue lake disappeared amid towering Alps. 'Locarno, sixty kilometres.'

'You don't say.' At the thought of Switzerland so close by, freedom swelled in Fidelman's heart but he did nothing about it. Scarpio clung to him like a long-lost brother and sixty kilometres was a long swim with a knife in your back.

'That's the castello over there,' the major domo said. 'It looks like a joint.'

The castello was pink on a high terraced hill amid tall trees in formal gardens. It was full of tourists and bad paintings. But in the last gallery, 'infinite riches in a little room', hung the 'Venus of Urbino' alone.

What a miracle, thought Fidelman.

The golden brown-haired Venus, a woman of the real world, lay on her couch in serene beauty, her hand lightly touching her intimate mystery, the other holding red flowers, her nude body her truest accomplishment.

'I would have painted somebody in bed with her,' Scarpio said.

'Shut up,' said Fidelman.

Scarpio, hurt, left the gallery.

Fidelman, alone with Venus, worshipped the painting. What magnificent tones, what extraordinary flesh that can turn the body into spirit.

While Scarpio was out talking to the guard, the copyist hastily sketched the Venus, and with a Leica Angelo had borrowed from a friend for the purpose, took several new colour shots.

Afterwards he approached the picture and kissed the lady's hands, thighs, and breasts, but as he was murmuring, 'I love you,' a guard struck him hard on the head with both fists.

That night as they returned on the rapido to Milano, Scarpio fell asleep, snoring. He awoke in a hurry, tugging at his dagger, but Fidelman hadn't moved.

2

The copyist threw himself into his work with passion. He had swallowed lightning and hoped it would strike whatever he touched. Yet he had nagging doubts he could do the job right and feared he would never escape alive from the Hôtel du Ville. He tried at once to paint the Titian directly on canvas but hurriedly scraped it clean when he saw what a garish mess he had made. The Venus was insanely disproportionate and the maids in the background foreshortened into dwarfs. He then took Angelo's advice and made several drawings on paper to master the composition before committing it again to canvas.

Angelo and Scarpio came up every night and shook their heads over the drawings.

'Not even close,' said the padrone.

'Far from it,' said Scarpio.

'I'm trying,' Fidelman said, anguished.

'Try harder,' Angelo said grimly.

Fidelman had a sudden insight. 'What happened to the last guy who tried?'

'He's still floating,' Scarpio said.

'I'll need some practice,' the copyist coughed. 'My vision seems tight and the arm tires easily. I'd better go back to some exercises to loosen up.'

'What kind of exercises?' Scarpio inquired.

'Nothing physical, just some warm-up nudes to get me going.'

'Don't overdo it,' Angelo said. 'You've got about a month, not much more. There's a certain advantage in making the exchange of pictures during the tourist season.'

'Only a month?'

The padrone nodded.

'Maybe you'd better trace it,' Scarpio said.

'No.'

'I'll tell you what,' said Angelo. 'I could get you an old reclining nude you could paint over. You might get the form of this one by altering the form of another.'

'No.'

'Why not?'

'It's not honest. I mean to myself.'

Everyone tittered.

'Well, it's your headache,' Angelo said.

Fidelman, unwilling to ask what happened if he failed, after they had left, feverishly drew faster.

Things went badly for the copyist. Working all day and often into the very early morning hours, he tried everything he could think of. Since he always distorted the figure of Venus, though he carried it perfect in his mind, he went back to a study of Greek statuary with ruler and compass to compute the mathematical proportions of the ideal nude. Scarpio accompanied him to one or two museums. Fidelman also worked with the Vitruvian square in the circle, experimented with Dürer's intersecting circles and triangles and studied Leonardo's schematic heads and bodies. Nothing doing. He

drew paper dolls, not women, certainly not Venus. He drew
girls who would not grow up. He then tried sketching every
nude he could lay eyes on in the art books Scarpio brought
him from the library, from the Esquiline goddess to 'Les
Demoiselles d'Avignon'. Fidelman copied not badly many
figures from classical statuary and modern painting, but
when he returned to his Venus, with something of a laugh
she eluded him. What am I, bewitched, the copyist asked
himself, and if so by what? It's only a copy job so what's
taking so long? He couldn't even guess until he happened to
see a naked whore cross the hall and enter a friend's room.
Maybe the ideal is cold and I like it hot? Nature over art?
Inspiration – the live model? Fidelman knocked on the
door and tried to persuade the girl to pose for him but she
wouldn't for economic reasons. Neither would any of the
others – there were four girls in the room.

A red-head among them called out to Fidelman, 'Shame
on you, Arturo, are you too good to bring up pizzas and
coffee any more?'

'I'm busy on a job for Angelo.'

The girls laughed.

'Painting a picture, that is. A business proposition.'

They laughed louder.

Their laughter further depressed his spirits. No inspiration
from whores. Maybe too many naked women around made
it impossible to draw a nude. Still he'd better try a live
model, having tried everything else and failed.

In desperation, practically on the verge of panic because
time was going so fast, he thought of Teresa, the chambermaid. She was a poor specimen of feminine beauty but the
imagination could enhance anything. Fidelman asked her to
pose for him, and Teresa, after a shy laugh, consented.

'I will if you promise not to tell anybody.'

Fidelman promised.

She got undressed, a meagre, bony girl, breathing heavily, and he drew her with flat chest, distended belly, thin hips and hairy legs, unable to alter a single detail. Van Eyck would have loved her. When Teresa saw the drawing she wept profusely.

'I thought you would make me beautiful.'

'I had that in mind.'

'Then why didn't you?'

'It's hard to say,' said Fidelman.

'I'm not in the least bit sexy,' she wept.

Considering her body with half-open eyes, Fidelman told her to go borrow a long slip.

'Get one from one of the girls and I'll draw you sexy.'

She returned in a frilly white slip and looked so attractive that instead of painting her, Fidelman, with a lump in his throat, got her to lie down with him on a dusty mattress in the room. Clasping her slip-encased form, the copyist shut both eyes and concentrated on his elusive Venus. He felt about to recapture a rapturous experience and was looking forward to it but at the last minute it turned into a limerick he didn't know he knew:

> 'Whilst Titian was mixing rose madder,
> His model was crouched on a ladder;
> Her position to Titian suggested coition,
> So he stopped mixing madder and had 'er.'

Angelo entering the storeroom just then, let out a furious bellow. He fired Teresa on her naked knees pleading with him not to, and Fidelman had to go back to latrine duty the rest of the day.

'You might just as well keep me doing this permanently,' Fidelman, disheartened, told the padrone in his office afterward. 'I'll never finish that cursed picture.'

'Why not? What's eating you? I've treated you like a son.'

'I'm blocked, that's what.'

'Get to work, you'll feel better.'

'I just can't paint.'

'For what reason?'

'I don't know.'

'Because you've had it too good here.' Angelo angrily struck Fidelman across the face. When the copyist wept, he booted him hard in the rear.

That night Fidelman went on a hunger strike but the padrone, hearing of it, threatened force feeding.

After midnight Fidelman stole some clothes from a sleeping whore, dressed quickly, tied on a kerchief, made up his eyes and lips, and walked out the door past Scarpio sitting on a bar stool, enjoying the night breeze. Having gone a block, fearing he would be chased, Fidelman broke into a high-heeled run but it was too late. Scarpio had recognized him in aftermath and called the portiere. Fidelman kicked off his slippers and ran furiously but the skirt impeded him. The major domo and portiere caught up with him and dragged him, kicking and struggling, back to the hotel. A carabiniere, hearing the commotion, appeared on the scene, but seeing how Fidelman was dressed, would do nothing for him. In the cellar Angelo hit him with a short rubber hose until he collapsed.

Fidelman lay in bed three days, refusing to eat or get up.

'What'll we do now?' Angelo, worried, whispered. 'How about a fortune teller? Either that or let's bury him.'

'Astrology is better,' Scarpio advised. 'I'll check his planets. If that doesn't work we'll try psychology.'

'Well, make it fast,' said Angelo.

The next morning Scarpio entered Fidelman's room with an American breakfast on a tray and two thick books under his arm. Fidelman was still in bed, smoking a butt. He wouldn't eat.

Scarpio set down his books and took a chair close to the bed.

'What's your birthday, Arturo?' he asked gently, feeling Fidelman's pulse.

Fidelman told him, also the hour of birth and the place: Bronx, New York.

Scarpio, consulting the zodiacal tables, drew up Fidelman's horoscope on a sheet of paper and studied it thoroughly with his good eye. After a few minutes he shook his head. 'It's no wonder.'

'What's wrong?' Fidelman sat up weakly.

'Your Uranus and Venus are both in bad shape.'

'My Venus?'

'She rules your fate.' He studied the chart. 'Taurus ascending. Venus afflicted. That's why you're blocked.'

'Afflicted by what?'

'Sh,' said Scarpio, 'I'm checking your Mercury.'

'Concentrate on Venus, when will she be better?'

Scarpio consulted the tables, jotted down some numbers and signs and slowly turned pale. He searched through a few more pages of tables, then got up and stared out the dirty window.

'It's hard to tell. Do you believe in psychoanalysis?'

'Sort of.'

'Maybe we'd better try that. Don't get up.'

Fidelman's head fell back on the pillow.

Scarpio opened a thick book to its first chapter. 'The thing to do is associate freely.'

'If I don't get out of this whorehouse soon I'll surely die,' said Fidelman.

'Do you have any memories of your mother?' Scarpio asked. 'For instance, did you ever see her naked?'

'She died at my birth,' Fidelman answered, on the verge of tears. 'I was raised by my sister Bessie.'

'Go on, I'm listening,' said Scarpio.

'I can't. My mind goes blank.'

Scarpio turned to the next chapter, flipped through several pages, then rose with a sigh.

'It might be a medical matter. Take a physic tonight.'

'I already have.'

The major domo shrugged. 'Life is complicated. Anyway, keep track of your dreams. Write them down as soon as you have them.'

Fidelman puffed his butt.

That night he dreamed of Bessie about to bathe. He was peeking at her through the bathroom keyhole as she was preparing her bath. Open mouthed he watched her remove her robe and step into the tub. Her hefty well-proportioned body then was young and full in the right places; and in the dream Fidelman, then fourteen, looked at her with longing that amounted to anguish. The older Fidelman, the dreamer, considered doing a 'La Baigneuse' right then and there, but when Bessie began to soap herself with Ivory soap, the boy slipped away into her room, opened her poor purse, filched fifty cents for the movies, and went on tiptoes down the stairs.

He was shutting the vestibule door with great relief when Arthur Fidelman woke with a headache. As he was scribbling down this dream he suddenly remembered what Angelo had said: 'Everybody steals. We're all human.'

A stupendous thought occurred to him: Suppose he personally were to steal the picture?

A marvellous idea all around. Fidelman heartily ate that morning's breakfast.

To steal the picture he had to paint one. Within another

day the copyist successfully sketched Titian's painting and then began to work in oils on an old piece of Flemish linen that Angelo had hastily supplied him with after seeing the successful drawing. Fidelman underpainted the canvas and after it was dry began the figure of Venus as the conspirators looked on sucking their breaths.

'Stay relaxed,' begged Angelo, sweating. 'Don't spoil it now. Remember you're painting the appearance of a picture. The original has already been painted. Give us a decent copy and we'll do the rest with chemistry.'

'I'm worried about the brush strokes.'

'Nobody will notice them. Just keep in your mind that Tiziano painted resolutely with few strokes, his brush loaded with colour. In the end he would paint with his fingers. Don't worry about that. We don't ask for perfection, just a good copy.'

He rubbed his fat fingers nervously.

But Fidelman painted as though he were painting the original. He worked alone late at night, when the conspirators were snoring, and he painted with what was left of his heart. He had caught the figure of the Venus but when it came to her flesh, her thighs and breasts, he never thought he would make it. As he painted he seemed to remember every nude that had ever been done, Fidelman satyr, with Silenus beard and goatlegs dancing among them, piping and peeking at backside, frontside, or both, at the 'Rokeby Venus', 'Bathsheba', 'Suzanna', 'Venus Anyomene', 'Olympia', at picknickers in dress or undress, bathers ditto, Vanitas or Truth, Niobe or Leda, in chase or embrace, hausfrau or whore, amorous ladies modest or brazen, single or in the crowds at the Turkish bath, in every conceivable shape or position, while he sported or disported until a trio of maenads pulled his curly beard and he galloped after them through the dusky woods. He was at the same time choked by remembered lust for all the women he had ever desired, from Bessie to Annamaria Oliovino, and for their garters, underpants, slips or half slips, brassieres and stockings. Although thus tormented, Fidelman felt himself falling in love with the one he painted, every inch of her, including the ring on her pinky, bracelet on arm, the flowers she touched with her fingers, and the bright green ear-ring that dangled from her eatable ear. He would have prayed her alive if he weren't certain she would fall in love, not with her famished creator, but surely the first Apollo Belvedere she laid eyes on. Is there, Fidelman asked himself, a world where love endures and is always satisfying? He answered in the negative. Still she was his as he painted, so he went on painting, planning never to finish, to be happy as he was in loving her, thus for ever happy.

But he finished the picture on Saturday night, Angelo's gun pressed to his head. Then the Venus was taken from him and Scarpio and Angelo baked, smoked, stippled and varnished, stretched and framed Fidelman's masterwork as the artist lay on his bed in his room in a state of collapse.

'The Venus of Urbino, c'est moi.'

3

'What about my three hundred and fifty?' Fidelman asked Angelo during a card game in the padrone's stuffy office several days later. After completing the painting the copyist was again back on janitorial duty.

'You'll collect when we've got the Tiziano.'

'I did my part.'

'Don't question decisions.'

'What about my passport?'

'Give it to him, Scarpio.'

Scarpio handed him the passport. Fidelman flipped through the booklet and saw all the pages were intact.

'If you skidoo now,' Angelo warned him. 'You'll get spit.'

'Who's skidooing?'

'So the plan is this: You and Scarpio will row out to the castello after midnight. The caretaker is an old man and half deaf. You hang our picture and breeze off with the other.'

'If you wish,' Fidelman suggested, 'I'll gladly do the job myself. Alone, that is.'

'Why alone?' said Scarpio suspiciously.

'Don't be foolish,' Angelo said. 'With the frame it weighs half a ton. Now listen to directions and don't give any. One reason I detest Americans is they never know their place.'

Fidelman apologized.

'I'll follow in the putt-putt and wait for you half-way between Isola Bella and Stresa in case we need a little extra speed at the last minute.'

'Do you expect trouble?'

'Not a bit. If there's any trouble it'll be your fault. In that case watch out.'

'Off with his head,' said Scarpio. He played a deuce and took the pot.

Fidelman laughed politely.

The next night, Scarpio rowed a huge weatherbeaten row-boat, both oars muffled. It was a moonless night with touches of Alpine lightning in the distant sky. Fidelman sat on the stern, holding with both hands and balancing against his knees the large framed painting, heavily wrapped in monk's cloth and cellophane, and tied around with rope.

At the island the major domo docked the boat and secured it. Fidelman, peering around in the dark, tried to memorize where they were. They carried the picture up two hundred steps, both puffing when they got to the formal gardens on top.

The castello was black except for a square of yellow light from the caretaker's turret window high above. As Scarpio snapped the lock of an embossed heavy wooden door with a strip of celluloid, the yellow window slowly opened and an old man peered down. They froze against the wall until the window was drawn shut.

'Fast,' Scarpio hissed. 'If anyone sees us they'll wake the whole island.'

Pushing open the creaking door, they quickly carried the painting, growing heavier as they hurried, through an enormous room cluttered with cheap statuary, and by the light of the major domo's flashlight, ascended a narrow flight of spiral stairs. They hastened in sneakers down a deep-shadowed, tapestried hall into the picture gallery, Fidelman stopping in his tracks when he beheld the Venus, the true and magnificent image of his counterfeit creation.

'Let's get to work.' Scarpio quickly unknotted the rope and they unwrapped Fidelman's painting and leaned it against the wall. They were taking down the Titian when footsteps sounded unmistakably in the hall. Scarpio's flashlight went out.

'Sh, it's the caretaker. If he comes in I'll have to conk him.'

'That'll destroy Angelo's plan – deceit, not force.'

'I'll think of that when we're out of here.'

They pressed their backs to the wall, Fidelman's clammy, as the old man's steps drew nearer. The copyist had anguished visions of losing the picture and made helter-skelter plans somehow to reclaim it. Then the footsteps faltered, came to a stop, and after a moment of intense hesitation, moved in another direction. A door slammed and the sound was gone.

It took Fidelman several seconds to breathe. They waited in the dark without moving until Scarpio shone his light. Both Venuses were resting against the same wall. The major domo closely inspected each canvas with one eye shut, then signalled the painting on the left. 'That's the one, let's wrap it up.'

Fidelman broke into profuse sweat.

'Are you crazy? That's mine. Don't you know a work of art when you see it?' He pointed to the other picture.

'Art?' said Scarpio, removing his hat and turning pale. 'Are you sure?' He peered at the painting.

'Without a doubt.'

'Don't try to confuse me.' He tapped the dagger under his coat.

'The lighter one is the Titian,' Fidelman said through a dry throat. 'You smoked mine a shade darker.'

'I could have sworn yours was the lighter.'

'No, Titian's. He used light varnishes. It's a historical fact.'

'Of course.' Scarpio mopped his brow with a soiled handkerchief. 'The trouble is with my eyes. One is in bad shape and I over-use the other.'

'Tst-tst,' clucked Fidelman.

'Anyway, hurry up. Angelo's waiting on the lake. Remember, if there's any mistake he'll cut your throat first.'

They hung the darker painting on the wall, quickly wrapped the lighter and hastily carried it through the long hall and down the stairs, Fidelman leading the way with Scarpio's light.

At the dock the major domo nervously turned to Fidelman. 'Are you absolutely sure we have the right one?'

'I give you my word.'

'I accept it but under the circumstances I'd better have another look. Shine the flashlight through your fingers.'

Scarpio knelt to undo the wrapping once more, and Fidelman, trembling, brought the flashlight down hard on Scarpio's straw hat, the light shattering in his hand. The major domo, pulling at his dagger, collapsed.

Fidelman had trouble loading the painting into the rowboat but finally got it in and settled, and quickly took off. In ten minutes he had rowed out of sight of the dark castled island. Not long afterward he thought he heard Angelo's putt-putt behind him, and his heart beat erratically, but the padrone did not appear. He rowed as the waves deepened.

Locarno, sixty kilometres.

A wavering flash of lightning pierced the broken sky, lighting the agitated lake all the way to the Alps, as a dreadful thought assailed Fidelman : had he the right painting, after all ? After a minute he pulled in his oars, listened once more for Angelo, and hearing nothing, stepped to the stern of the rowboat, letting it drift as he frantically unwrapped the Venus.

In the pitch black, on the lake's choppy waters, he saw she was indeed his, and by the light of numerous matches adored his handiwork.

The Cost of Living

Winter had fled the city streets but Sam Tomashevsky's face, when he stumbled into the back room of his grocery store, was a blizzard. Sura, who was sitting at the round table eating bread and salted tomato, looked up in fright and the tomato turned a deeper red. She gulped the bite she had bitten and with pudgy fist socked her chest to make it go down. The gesture already was one of mourning for she knew from the wordless sight of him there was trouble.

'My God,' Sam croaked.

She screamed, making him shudder, and he fell wearily into a chair. Sura was standing, enraged and frightened.

'Speak, for God's sake.'

'Next door,' Sam muttered.

'What happened next door?' – upping her voice.

'Comes a store!'

'What kind of a store?' The cry was piercing.

He waved his arms in rage. 'A grocery comes next door.'

'Oi.' She bit her knuckle and sank down moaning. It could not have been worse.

They had, all winter, been haunted by the empty store. An Italian shoemaker had owned it for years and then a streamlined shoe-repair shop had opened up next block where they had three men in red smocks hammering away in the window and everyone stopped to look. Pellegrino's business had slackened off as if someone were shutting a faucet, and one day he had looked at his workbench and when everything stopped jumping, it loomed up ugly and empty. All morning he had sat motionless, but in the after-noon he put down the hammer he had been clutching and got his jacket and an old darkened Panama hat a customer had never called for when he used to do hat cleaning and blocking; then he went into the neighbourhood, asking among his former customers for work they might want done. He collected two pairs of shoes, a man's brown and white ones for summer-time and a fragile pair of ladies' dancing slippers. At the same time, Sam found his own soles and heels had been worn paper thin for being so many hours on his feet – he could feel the cold floor boards under him as he walked – and that made three pairs all together, which was what Mr Pellegrino had that week – and another pair the week after. When the time came for him to pay next month's rent he sold everything to a junkman and bought candy to peddle with in the streets; but after a while no one saw the shoemaker any more, a stocky man with round eyeglasses and a bristling moustache, wearing a sum-mer hat in wintertime.

When they tore up the counters and other fixtures and moved them out, when the store was empty except for the sink glowing in the rear, Sam would occasionally stand there at night, everyone on the block but him closed, peering into the window exuding darkness. Often, while gazing through the dusty plate glass, which gave him back the image of a grocer gazing out, he felt as he had when he was a boy in Kamenets-Podolskiy and going, three of them, to the river; they would, as they passed, swoop a frightened glance into a tall wooden house, eerily narrow, topped by a strange double-steepled roof, where there had once been a ghastly murder and now the place was haunted. Returning late, at times in early moonlight, they walked a distance away, speechless, listening to the ravenous silence of the house, room after room fallen into deeper stillness, and in the midmost a pit of churning quiet from which, if you thought about it, all evil erupted. And so it seemed in the dark recesses of the empty store, where so many shoes had been leathered and hammered into life, and so many people had left something of themselves in the coming and going, that even in emptiness the store contained some memory of their vanished presences, unspoken echoes in declining tiers, and that in a sense was what was so frightening. Afterwards when Sam went by the store, even in daylight he was afraid to look, and quickly walked past, as they had the haunted house when he was a boy.

But whenever he shut his eyes the empty store was stuck in his mind, a long black hole eternally revolving so that while he slept he was not asleep but within revolving : what if it should happen to me ? What if after twenty-seven years of eroding toil (he should years ago have got out), what if after all of that, your own store, a place of business . . . after all the years, the years, the multitude of cans he had wiped off and packed away, the milk cases dragged in like rocks from the street before dawn in freeze or heat ; insults, petty thievery, doling of credit to the impoverished by the poor ; the peeling ceiling, fly-specked shelves, puffed cans, dirt, swollen veins ; the back-breaking sixteen-hour day like a heavy hand slapping, upon awakening, the skull, pushing the head to bend the body's bones ; the hours ; the work, the years, my God, and where is my life now ? Who will save me now, and where will I go, where ? Often he had thought these thoughts, subdued after months ; and the garish FOR RENT sign had yellowed and fallen in the window so how could any one know the place was to let ? But they did. Today when he had all but laid the ghost of fear, a streamer in red cracked him across the eyes : National Grocery Will Open Another Of Its Bargain Price Stores On These Premises, and the woe went into him and his heart bled.

At last Sam raised his head and told her, 'I will go to the landlord next door.'

Sura looked at him through puffy eyelids. 'So what will you say?'

'I will talk to him.'

Ordinarily she would have said, 'Sam, don't be a fool,' but she let him go.

Averting his head from the glare of the new red sign in the window, he entered the hall next door. As he laboured up the steps the bleak light from the skylight fell on him and grew heavier as he ascended. He went unwillingly, not knowing what he would say to the landlord. Reaching the top floor he paused before the door at the jabbering in Italian of a woman bewailing her fate. Sam already had one foot on the top stair, ready to descend, when he heard the coffee advertisement and realized it had been a radio play. Now the radio was off, the hallway oppressively silent. He listened and at first heard no voices inside so he knocked without allowing himself to think any more. He was a little frightened and lived in suspense until the slow heavy steps of the landlord, who was also the barber across the street, reached the door, and it was – after some impatient fumbling with the lock – opened.

When the barber saw Sam in the hall he was disturbed, and Sam at once knew why he had not been in the store even once in the past two weeks. However, the barber became cordial and invited Sam to step into the kitchen where his wife and a stranger were seated at the table eating from piled-high plates of spaghetti.

'Thanks,' said Sam shyly. 'I just ate.'

The barber came out into the hall, shutting the door behind them. He glanced vaguely down the stairway and then turned to Sam. His movements were unresolved. Since the death of his son in the war he had become absent-minded;

THE COST OF LIVING

and sometimes when he walked one had the impression he was dragging something.

'Is it true?' Sam asked in embarrassment, 'What it says downstairs on the sign?'

'Sam,' the barber began heavily. He stopped to wipe his mouth with the napkin he held in his hand and said, 'Sam, you know this store I had no rent for it for seven months?'

'I know.'

'I can't afford. I was waiting for maybe a liquor store or a hardware but I don't have no offers from them. Last month this chain-store make me an offer and then I wait five weeks for something else. I had to take it, I couldn't help my-self.'

Shadows thickened in the growing darkness. In a sense Pellegrino was present, standing with them at the top of the stairs.

'When will they move in?' Sam sighed.

'Not till May.'

The grocer was too faint to say anything. They stared at each other, not knowing what to suggest. But the barber forced a laugh and said the chain-store wouldn't hurt Sam's business.

'Why not?'

'Because you carry different brands of goods and when the customers want those brands they go to you.'

'Why should they go to me if my prices are higher?'

'A chain-store brings more customers and they might like things that you got.'

Sam felt ashamed. He didn't doubt the barber's sincerity but his stock was meagre and he could not imagine chain-store customers interested in what he had to sell.

Holding Sam by the arm, the barber told him in confidential tones of a friend who had a meat store next to an A & P Supermarket and was making out very well.

Sam tried hard to believe he would make out well but couldn't.

'So did you sign with them the lease yet?' he asked.

'Friday,' said the barber.

'Friday?' Sam had a wild hope. 'Maybe,' he said, trying to hold it down, 'maybe I could find you, before Friday, a new tenant?'

'What kind of a tenant?'

'A tenant,' Sam said.

'What kind of store is he interested?'

Sam tried to think. 'A shoe store,' he said.

'Shoemaker?'

'No, a shoe store where they sell shoes.'

The barber pondered it. At last he said if Sam could get a tenant he wouldn't sign the lease with the chain-store.

As Sam descended the stairs the light from the top-floor bulb diminished on his shoulders but not the heaviness, for he had no one in mind to take the store.

However, before Friday he thought of two people. One was the red-haired salesman for a wholesale grocery jobber, who had lately been recounting his investments in new stores; but when Sam spoke to him on the phone he said he was only interested in high-income grocery stores, which was no solution to the problem. The other man he hesitated to call, because he didn't like him. That was I. Kaufman, a former dry-goods merchant, with a wart under his left eyebrow. Kaufman had made some fortunate real estate deals and had become quite wealthy. Years ago he and Sam had stores next to one another on Marcy Avenue in Williamsburg. Sam took him for a lout and was not above saying so, for which Sura often ridiculed him, seeing how Kaufman had progressed and where Sam was. Yet they stayed on comparatively good terms, perhaps because the grocer never asked for favours. When Kaufman happened to be around in the Buick, he usually dropped in, which Sam increasingly disliked, for Kaufman gave advice without stint and Sura sandpapered it in when he had left.

Despite qualms he telephoned him. Kaufman was pontifically surprised and said yes he would see what he could do. On Friday morning the barber took the red sign out of the window so as not to prejudice a possible deal. When Kaufman marched in with his cane that forenoon, Sam, who for once, at Sura's request, had dispensed with his apron, explained to him they had thought of the empty store next door as perfect for a shoe store because the neighbourhood had none and the rent was reasonable. And since Kaufman was always investing in one project or another they thought he might be interested in this. The barber came over from across the street and unlocked the door. Kaufman clomped into the empty store, appraised the structure of the place, tested the floor, peered through the barred window into the back yard, and squinting, totalled with moving lips how much shelving was necessary and at what cost. Then he asked the barber how much rent and the barber named a modest figure.

Kaufman nodded sagely and said nothing to either of them there, but back in the grocery store he vehemently berated Sam for wasting his time.

'I didn't want to make you ashamed in front of the goy,' he said in anger, even his wart red, 'but who do you think, if he is in his right mind, will open a shoe store in this stinky neighbourhood?'

Before departing, he gave good advice the way a tube bloops toothpaste and ended by saying to Sam, 'If a chainstore grocery comes in you're finished. Get out of here before the birds pick the meat out of your bones.'

Then he drove off in his Buick. Sura was about to begin a commentary but Sam pounded his fist on the table and that ended it. That evening the barber pasted the red sign back on the window, for he had signed the lease.

Lying awake nights, Sam knew what was going on inside the store, though he never went near it. He could see carpenters sawing the sweet-smelling pine that willingly yielded to the sharp shining blade and became in tiers the shelves rising to the ceiling. The painters arrived, a long man and a short one he was positive he knew, their faces covered with paint drops. They thickly calcimined the ceiling and painted everything in bright colours, impractical for a grocery but pleasing to the eye. Electricians appeared with fluorescent lamps which obliterated the yellow darkness of globed bulbs; and then the fixture men hauled down from their vans the long marble-top counters and a gleaming enamelled refrigerator containing three windows, for cooking, medium, and best butter; and a case of frozen foods, creamy white, the latest thing. As he was admiring it all, he thought he turned to see if anyone was watching him, and when he had reassured himself and turned again to look through the window it had been whitened so he could see nothing more. He had to get up then to smoke a cigarette and was tempted to put on his pants and go in slippers quietly down the stairs to see if the window was really soaped. That it might be kept him back so he returned to bed, and being still unable to sleep, he worked until he had polished, with a bit of rag, a small hole in the centre of the white window, and enlarged that till he could see everything clearly. The store was assembled now, spic and span, roomy, ready to receive the goods; it was a pleasure to come in. He whispered to himself this would be good if it was for me, but then the alarm banged in his ear and he had to get up and drag in the milk cases. At eight a.m. three enormous trucks rolled down the block and six young men in white duck jackets jumped off and packed the store in seven hours. All day

Sam's heart beat so hard he sometimes fondled it with his hand as though trying to calm a wild bird that wanted to fly away.

When the chain-store opened in the middle of May, with a horseshoe wreath of roses in the window, Sura counted up that night and proclaimed they were ten dollars short; which wasn't so bad, Sam said, till she reminded him ten times six was sixty. She openly wept, sobbing they must do *something*, driving Sam to a thorough wiping of the shelves with wet clothes she handed him, oiling the floor, and washing, inside and out, the front window, which she redecorated with white tissue paper from the five-and-ten. Then she told him to call the wholesaler, who read off this week's specials; and when they were delivered, Sam packed three cases of cans in a towering pyramid in the window. Only no one seemed to buy. They were fifty dollars short the next week and Sam thought if it stays like this we can exist, and he cut the price of beer, lettering with black crayon on wrapping paper a sign for the window that beer was reduced in price, selling fully five cases more that day, though Sura nagged what was the good of it if they made no profit – lost on paper bags – and the customers who came in for beer went next door for bread and canned goods? Yet Sam still hoped, but the next week they were seventy-two behind, and in two weeks a clean hundred. The chain-store, with a manager and two clerks, was busy all day but with Sam there was never, any more, anything resembling a rush. Then he discovered that they carried, next door, every brand he had and many he hadn't, and he felt for the barber a furious anger.

That summer, usually better for his business, was bad, and the fall was worse. The store was so silent it got to be a piercing pleasure when someone opened the door. They sat long hours under the unshaded bulb in the rear, reading and rereading the newspaper and looking up hopefully when anyone passed by in the street, though trying not to look when they could tell he was going next door. Sam now kept open an hour longer, till midnight, although that wearied him greatly, but he was able, during the extra hour, to pick up a dollar or two among the housewives who had run out of milk or needed a last-minute loaf of bread for school sandwiches. To cut expenses he put out one of the two lights in the window and a lamp in the store. He had the phone removed, bought his paper bags from pedlars, shaved every second day and, although he would not admit it, ate less. Then in an unexpected burst of optimism he ordered eighteen cases of goods from the jobber and filled the empty sections of his shelves with low-priced items clearly marked, but as Sura said, who saw them if nobody came in? People he had seen every day for ten, fifteen, even twenty years, disappeared as if they had moved or died. Sometimes when he was delivering a small order somewhere, he saw a former customer who either quickly crossed the street, or ducked the other way and walked around the block. The barber, too, avoided him and he avoided the barber. Sam schemed to give short weight on loose items but couldn't bring himself to. He considered canvassing the neighbourhood from house to house for orders he would personally deliver but then remembered Mr Pellegrino and gave up the idea. Sura, who had all their married life nagged him, now sat silent in the back. When Sam counted the receipts for the first week in December he knew he could no longer hope. The wind blew outside and the store was cold. He offered it for sale but no one would take it.

One morning Sura got up and slowly ripped her cheeks with her fingernails. Sam went across the street for a haircut. He had formerly had his hair cut once a month but now it had grown ten weeks and was thickly pelted at the back of the neck. The barber cut it with his eyes shut. Then Sam called an auctioneer who moved in with two lively assistants and a red auction flag that flapped and furled in the icy breeze as though it were a holiday. The money they got was not a quarter of the sum needed to pay the creditors. Sam and Sura closed the store and moved away. So long as he lived he would not return to the old neighbourhood, afraid his store was standing empty, and he dreaded to look through the window.

The Maid's Shoes

The maid had left her name with the porter's wife. She said she was looking for steady work and would take anything but preferred not to work for an old woman. Still if she had to she would. She was forty-five and looked older. Her face was worn but her hair was black, and her eyes and lips were pretty. She had few good teeth. When she laughed she was embarrassed around the mouth. Although it was cold in early October, that year in Rome, and the chestnut vendors were already bent over their pans of glowing charcoals, the maid wore only a threadbare black cotton dress which had a split down the left side, where about two inches of seam had opened on the hip, exposing her underwear. She had sewn the seam several times but this was one of the times it was open again. Her heavy but well-formed legs were bare and she wore house slippers as she talked to the portinaia; she had done a single day's washing for a signora down the street and carried her shoes in a paper bag. There were three comparatively new apartment houses on the hilly street and she left her name in each of them.

The portinaia, a dumpy woman wearing a brown tweed skirt she had got from an English family that had once lived in the building, said she would remember the maid but then she forgot; she forgot until an American professor moved into a furnished apartment on the fifth floor and asked her to help him find a maid. The portinaia brought him a girl from the neighbourhood, a girl of sixteen, recently from Umbria, who came with her aunt. But the professor, Orlando Krantz, did not like the way the aunt played

up certain qualities of the girl, so he sent her away. He told
the portinaia he was looking for an older woman, someone
he wouldn't have to worry about. Then the portinaia
thought of the maid who had left her name and address, and
she went to her house on the via Appia Antica near the cata-
combs and told her an American was looking for a maid,
mezzo servizio; she would give him her name if the maid
agreed to make it worth her while. The maid, whose name
was Rosa, shrugged her shoulders and looked stiffly down
the street. She said she had nothing to offer the portinaia.

'Look at what I'm wearing,' she said. 'Look at this junk
pile, can you call it a house? I live here with my son and his
bitch of a wife who counts every spoonful of soup in my
mouth. They treat me like dirt and dirt is all I have to my
name.'

'In that case I can do nothing for you,' the portinaia said.
'I have myself and my husband to think of.' But she returned from the bus stop and said she would recommend
the maid to the American professor if she gave her five
thousand lire the first time she was paid.

'How much will he pay?' the maid asked the portinaia.

'I would ask for eighteen thousand a month. Tell him you
have to spend two hundred lire a day for carfare.'

'That's almost right,' Rosa said. 'It will cost me forty
one way and forty back. But if he pays me eighteen thous-
and I'll give you five if you sign that's all I owe you.'

'I will sign,' said the portinaia, and she recommended the
maid to the American professor.

Orlando Krantz was a nervous man of sixty. He had mild
grey eyes, a broad mouth, and a pointed clefted chin. His
round head was bald and he had a bit of a belly, although
the rest of him was quite thin. He was a somewhat odd-
looking man but an authority in law, the portinaia told
Rosa. The professor sat at a table in his study, writing all

day, yet was up every half hour on some pretext or other to look nervously around. He worried how things were going and often came out of his study to see. He would watch Rosa working, then went in and wrote. In a half hour he would come out, ostensibly to wash his hands in the bathroom or drink a glass of water, but he was really passing by to see what she was doing. She was doing what she had to. Rosa worked quickly, especially when he was watching. She seemed, he thought, to be unhappy, but that was none of his business. Their lives, he knew, were full of troubles, often sordid; it was best to be detached.

This was the professor's second year in Italy; he had spent the first in Milan, and the second was in Rome. He had rented a large three-bedroom apartment, one of which he used as a study. His wife and daughter, who had returned for a visit to the States in August, would have the other bedrooms; they were due back before not too long. When the ladies returned, he had told Rosa, he would put her on full time. There was a maid's room where she could sleep; indeed, which she already used as her own though she was in the apartment only from nine till four. Rosa agreed to a full-time arrangement because it would mean all her meals in and no rent to pay her son and his dog-faced wife.

While they were waiting for Mrs Krantz and the daughter to arrive, Rosa did the marketing and cooking. She made the professor's breakfast when she came in, and his lunch at one. She offered to stay later than four, to prepare his supper, which he ate at six, but he preferred to take that meal out. After shopping she cleaned the house, thoroughly mopping the marble floors with a wet rag she pushed around with a stick though the floors did not look particularly dusty to him. She also washed and ironed his laundry. She was a good worker, her slippers clip-clopping as she hurried from one room to the next, and she frequently finished up about an hour or so before she was due to go home; so she retired to the maid's room and there read *Tempo* or *Epoca*, or sometimes a love story in photographs, with the words printed in italics under each picture. Often she pulled her bed down and lay in it under blankets, to keep warm. The weather had turned rainy, and now the apartment was uncomfortably cold. The custom of the condominium in this apartment house was not to heat until the fifteenth of November, and if it was cold before then, as it was now, the people of the house had to do the best they could. The cold disturbed the professor, who wrote with his gloves and hat on, and increased his nervousness so that he was out to look at her more often. He wore a heavy blue bathrobe over his clothes; sometimes the bathrobe belt was wrapped around a hot water bottle he had placed against the lower part of his back, under the suit coat. Sometimes he sat on the hot water bag as he wrote, a sight that caused Rosa, when she once saw this, to smile behind her hand. If he left the hot water bag in the dining-room after lunch, Rosa asked if she might use it. As a rule he allowed her to, and then she did her work with the rubber bag pressed against her stomach with her elbow. She said she had trouble with her liver. That was why the professor did not mind her going to the maid's room to lie down before leaving, after she had finished her work.

Once after Rosa had gone home, smelling tobacco smoke in the corridor near her room, the professor entered it to investigate. The room was not more than an elongated cubicle with a narrow bed that lifted sideways against the wall; there was also a small green cabinet, and an adjoining tiny bathroom containing a toilet and a sitzbath fed by a cold-water tap. She often did the laundry on a washboard in the sitzbath, but never, so far as he knew, had bathed in it. The day before her daughter-in-law's name day she had asked permission to take a hot bath in his tub in the big bathroom, and though he had hesitated a moment, the professor finally said yes. In her room, he opened a drawer at the bottom of the cabinet and found a hoard of cigarette butts in it, the butts he had left in ash trays. He noticed, too, that she had collected his old newspapers and magazines from the waste baskets. She also saved cord, paper bags and rubber bands; also pencil stubs he threw away. After he found that out, he occasionally gave her some meat left over from lunch, and cheese that had gone dry, to take with her. For this she brought him flowers. She also brought a dirty egg or two her daughter-in-law's hen had laid, but he thanked her and said the yolks were too strong for his taste. He noticed that she needed a pair of shoes, for those she put on to go home in were split in several places, and she wore the same black dress with the tear in it every day, which embarrassed him when he had to speak to her; however, he thought he would refer these matters to his wife when she arrived.

As jobs went, Rosa knew she had a good one. The professor paid well and promptly, and he never ordered her around in the haughty manner of some of her Italian employers. This one was nervous and fussy but not a bad sort. His main fault was his silence. Though he could speak a better than passable Italian, he preferred, when not at work, to sit in an armchair in the living-room, reading. Only two souls in the whole apartment, you would think they would want to talk to each other once in a while. Sometimes when she served him a cup of coffee as he read, she tried to get in a word about her troubles. She wanted to tell him about her long, impoverished widowhood, how badly her son had turned out, and what her miserable daughter-in-law was to live with. But though he listened courteously; though they shared the same roof, and even the same hot water bottle and bathtub, they almost never shared speech. He said no more to her than a crow would, and clearly showed he preferred to be left alone. So she left him alone and was lonely in the apartment. Working for foreigners had its advantages, she thought, but it also had disadvantages.

After a while the professor noticed that the telephone was ringing regularly for Rosa each afternoon during the time she usually was resting in her room. In the following week, instead of staying in the house until four, after her telephone call she asked permission to leave. At first she said her liver was bothering her, but later she stopped giving excuses. Although he did not much approve of this sort of thing, suspecting she would take advantage of him if he was too liberal in granting favours, he informed her that, until his wife arrived, she might leave at three on two afternoons of the week, provided that all her duties were fully discharged. He knew that everything was done before she left but thought he ought to say it. She listened meekly – her eyes aglow, lips twitching – and meekly agreed. He presumed, when he happened to think about it afterwards, that Rosa had a good spot here, by any standard, and she ought soon to show it in her face, change her unhappy expression for one less so. However, this did not happen, for when he chanced to observe her, even on days when she was leaving early, she seemed sadly preoccupied, sighed much, as if something on her heart were weighing her down.

He never asked what, preferring not to become involved in whatever it was. These people had endless troubles, and if you let yourself get involved in them you got endlessly involved. He knew of one woman, the wife of a colleague, who had said to her maid : 'Lucrezia, I am sympathetic to your condition but I don't want to hear about it.' This, the professor reflected, was basically good policy. It kept employer-employee relationships where they belonged – on an objective level. He was, after all, leaving Italy in April and would never in his life see Rosa again. It would do her a lot more good if, say, he sent her a small cheque at Christmas, than if he needlessly immersed himself in her miseries now. The professor knew he was nervous and often impatient, and he was sometimes sorry for his nature; but he was what he was and preferred to stay aloof from what did not closely and personally concern him.

But Rosa would not have it so. One morning she knocked on his study door, and when he said avanti, she went in embarrassedly so that even before she began to speak he was himself embarrassed.

'Professore,' Rosa said, unhappily, 'please excuse me for bothering your work, but I have to talk to somebody.'

'I happen to be very busy,' he said, growing a little angry. 'Can it wait a while?'

'It'll take only a minute. Your troubles hang on all your life but it doesn't take long to tell them.'

'Is it your liver complaint?' he asked.

'No. I need your advice. You're an educated man and I'm no more than an ignorant peasant.'

'What kind of advice?' he asked impatiently.

'Call it anything you like. The fact is I have to speak to somebody. I can't talk to my son, even if it were possible in this case. When I open my mouth he roars like a bull. And my daughter-in-law isn't worth wasting my breath on. Sometimes, on the roof, when we're hanging the wash, I say a few words to the portinaia, but she isn't a sympathetic person so I have to come to you, I'll tell you why.'

Before he could say how he felt about hearing her confidences, Rosa had launched into a story about this middle-aged government worker in the tax bureau, whom she had happened to meet in the neighbourhood. He was married, had four children, and sometimes worked as a carpenter after leaving his office at two o'clock each day. His name

was Armando; it was he who telephoned her every afternoon. They had met recently on a bus, and he had, after two
or three meetings, seeing that her shoes weren't fit to wear,
urged her to let him buy her a new pair. She had told him
not to be foolish. One could see he had very little, and it was
enough that he took her to the movies twice a week. She had
said that, yet every time they met he talked about the shoes
he wanted to buy her.

'I'm only human,' Rosa frankly told the professor, 'and
I need the shoes badly, but you know how these things go.
If I put on his shoes they may carry me to his bed. That's
why I thought I would ask you if I ought to take them.'

The professor's face and bald head were flushed. 'I don't
see how I can possibly advise you –'

'You're the educated one,' she said.

'However,' he went on, 'since the situation is still essenti-
ally hypothetical, I will go so far as to say you ought to tell
this generous gentleman that his responsibilities should be to
his own family. He would do well not to offer you gifts, as
you will do, not to accept them. If you don't, he can't possibly make any claims upon you or your person. This is all I
care to say. Your business is certainly none of mine. Since
you have requested advice, I've given it, but I won't say any
more.'

Rosa sighed. 'The truth of it is I could use a pair of shoes.
Mine look as though they've been chewed by goats. I haven't
had a new pair in six years.'

But the professor had nothing more to add.

After Rosa had gone for the day, in thinking about her
problem, he decided to buy her a pair of shoes. He was con-
cerned that she might be expecting something of the sort,
had planned, so to speak, to have it work out this way. But
since this was conjecture only, evidence entirely lacking, he
would assume, until proof to the contrary became available,

that she had no ulterior motive in asking his advice. He considered giving her five thousand lire to make the purchase of the shoes herself and relieve him of the trouble, but he was doubtful for there was no guarantee she would use the money for the agreed purpose. Suppose she came in the next day, saying she had had a liver attack that had necessitated calling the doctor, who had charged three thousand lire for his visit; therefore would the professor, in view of these unhappy circumstances, supply an additional three thousand for the shoes? That would never do, so the next morning, when the maid was at the grocer's, the professor slipped into her room and quickly traced on paper the outline of her miserable shoe – a distasteful task but he accomplished it quickly. That evening, in a store on the same piazza as the restaurant where he liked to eat, he bought Rosa a pair of brown shoes for fifty-five hundred lire, slightly more than he had planned to spend; but they were a solid pair of ties, walking shoes with a medium heel, a practical gift.

He gave them to Rosa the next day, a Wednesday. He felt a bit embarrassed to be doing that, because he realized that, despite his warnings to her, he had permitted himself to meddle in her affairs; but he considered giving her the shoes a psychologically proper move in more ways than one. In presenting her with them he said, 'Rosa, I have perhaps a solution to suggest in the matter you discussed with me. Here are a pair of new shoes for you. Tell your friend you must refuse his. And when you do, perhaps it would be advisable also to inform him that you intend to see him a little less frequently from now on.'

Rosa was overjoyed at the professor's kindness. She attempted to kiss his hand but he thrust it behind him and at once retired to his study. On Thursday, when he opened the apartment door to her ring, she was wearing his shoes. She carried a large paper bag from which she offered the professor three small oranges still on a branch with green leaves. He said she needn't have bought them but Rosa, smiling half hiddenly in order not to show her teeth, said that she wanted him to see how grateful she was. Later she requested permission to leave at three so she could show Armando her new shoes.

He said dryly, 'You may go at that hour if your work is done.'

She thanked him profusely. Hastening through her tasks, she left shortly after three, but not before the professor, in his hat, gloves and bathrobe, standing nervously at his open study door as he was inspecting the corridor floor she had just mopped, saw her hurrying out of the apartment, wearing a pair of dressy black needlepoint pumps. This angered him; and when Rosa appeared the next morning, though she begged him not to when he said she had made a fool of him and he was firing her to teach her a lesson, the professor did. She wept, pleading for another chance, but he would not change his mind. So she desolately wrapped up the odds and ends in her room in a newspaper and left, still crying. Afterwards he was upset and very nervous. He could not stand the cold that day and he could not work.

A week later, the morning the heat was turned on, Rosa appeared at the apartment door, and begged to have her job back. She was distraught, said her son had hit her, and gently touched her puffed black-and-blue upper lip. With tears in her eyes, although she didn't cry, Rosa explained it was no fault of hers that she had accepted both pairs of shoes. Armando had given her his pair first; had, out of jealousy of a possible rival, forced her to take them. Then when the professor had kindly offered his pair of shoes, she had wanted to refuse them but was afraid of angering him and losing her job. This was God's truth, so help her St Peter. She would, she promised, find Armando, whom she had not seen in a week, and return his shoes if the professor would take her back. If he didn't, she would throw herself into the Tiber. He, though he didn't care for talk of this kind, felt a certain sympathy for her. He was disappointed in himself at the way he had handled her. It would have been better to have said a few appropriate words on the subject of honesty and then philosophically dropped the matter. In firing her he had only made things difficult for them both, because, in the meantime he had tried two other maids and found them unsuitable. One stole, the other was lazy. As a result the house was a mess, impossible for him to work in, although the portinaia came up for an hour each morning to clean. It was his good fortune that Rosa had appeared at the door just then. When she removed her coat, he noticed with satisfaction that the tear in her dress had finally been sewn.

She went grimly to work, dusting, polishing, cleaning everything in sight. She unmade beds, then made them, swept under them, mopped, polished head and foot boards, adorned the beds with newly pressed spreads. Though she had just got her job back and worked with her usual efficiency, she worked, he observed, in sadness, frequently sighing, attempting a smile only when his eye was on her. This is their nature, he thought; they have hard lives. To spare her further blows by her son he gave her permission to live in. He offered extra money to buy meat for her supper but she refused it, saying pasta would do. Pasta and green salad was all she ate at night. Occasionally she boiled an artichoke left over from lunch and ate it with oil and vinegar. He invited her to drink the white wine in the cupboard and take fruit. Once in a while she did, always telling what and how much, though he repeatedly asked her not to. The apartment was nicely in order. Though the phone rang, as usual, daily at three, only seldom did she leave the house after she had talked with Armando.

Then one dismal morning Rosa came to the professor and in her distraught way confessed she was pregnant. Her face was lit in despair; her white underwear shone through her black dress.

He felt disgust, blaming himself for having re-employed her.

'You must leave at once,' he said, trying to keep his voice from trembling.

'I can't,' she said. 'My son will kill me. In God's name, help me, professore.'

He was infuriated by her stupidity. 'Your adventures are none of my responsibility.'

'You've got to help me,' she moaned.

'Was it this Armando?' he asked almost savagely.

She nodded.

'Have you informed him?'

'Yes.'

'What did he say?'

'He says he can't believe it.' She tried to smile but couldn't.

'I'll convince him,' he said. 'Do you have his telephone number?'

She told it to him. He called Armando at his office, identified himself, and asked the government clerk to come at once to the apartment. 'You have a grave responsibility to Rosa.'

'I have a grave responsibility to my family,' Armando answered.

'You might have considered them before this.'

'All right, I'll come over tomorrow after work. It's impossible today. I have a carpentering contract to finish up.'

'She'll expect you,' the professor said.

When he hung up he felt less angry, though still more

emotional than he cared to feel. 'Are you quite sure of your condition?' he asked her, 'that you are pregnant?'

'Yes.' She was crying now. 'Tomorrow is my son's birthday. What a beautiful present it will be for him to find out his mother's a whore. He'll break my bones, if not with his hands, then with his teeth.'

'It hardly seems likely you can conceive, considering your age.'

'My mother gave birth at fifty.'

'Isn't there a possibility you are mistaken?'

'I don't know. It's never been this way before. After all, I've been a widow –'

'Well, you'd better find out.'

'Yes, I want to,' Rosa said. 'I want to see the midwife in my neighbourhood but I haven't got a single lire. I spent all I had left when I wasn't working, and I had to borrow carfare to get here. Armando can't help me just now. He has to pay for his wife's teeth this week. She has very bad teeth, poor thing. That's why I came to you. Could you advance me two thousand of my pay so I can be examined by the midwife?'

I must put an end to this, he thought. After a minute he counted two one-thousand-lire notes out of his wallet. 'Go to her now,' he said. He was about to add that if she was pregnant, not to come back, but he was afraid she might do something desperate, or lie to him so she could go on working. He didn't want her around any more. When he thought of his wife and daughter arriving amidst this mess, he felt sick with nervousness. He wanted to get rid of the maid as soon as possible.

The next day Rosa came in at twelve instead of nine. Her dark face was pale. 'Excuse me for being late,' she murmured. 'I was praying at my husband's grave.'

'That's all right,' the professor said. 'But did you go to the midwife?'

'Not yet.'

'Why not?' Though angry he spoke calmly.

She stared at the floor.

'Please answer my question.'

'I was going to say I lost the two thousand lire on the bus, but after being at my husband's grave I'll tell you the truth. After all, it's bound to come out.'

This is terrible, he thought, it's unending. 'What did you do with the money?'

'That's what I mean,' Rosa sighed. 'I bought my son a present. Not that he deserves it but it was his birthday.' She burst into tears.

He stared at her a minute, then said, 'Please come with me.'

The professor left the apartment in his bathrobe, and Rosa followed. Opening the elevator door he stepped inside, holding the door for her. She entered the elevator.

They stopped two floors below. He got out and near-sightedly scanned the names on the brass plates above the bells. Finding the one he wanted, he pressed the button. A maid opened the door and let them in. She seemed frightened at Rosa's expression.

'Is the doctor in?' the professor asked the doctor's maid.

'I will see.'

'Please ask him if he'll see me for a minute. I live in the building, two flights up.'

'Si, signore.' She glanced again at Rosa, then went inside.

The Italian doctor came out, a short middle-aged man with a beard. The professor had once or twice passed him in the cortile of the apartment house. The doctor was buttoning his shirt cuff.

'I am sorry to trouble you, sir,' said the professor. 'This is my maid, who has been having some difficulty. She would like to determine whether she is pregnant. Can you assist her?'

The doctor looked at him, then at the maid, who had a handkerchief to her eyes.

'Let her come into my office.'

'Thank you,' said the professor. The doctor nodded.

The professor went up to his apartment. In a half hour the phone rang.

'Pronto.'

It was the doctor. 'She is not pregnant,' he said. 'She is frightened. She also has trouble with her liver.'

'Can you be certain, doctor?'

'Yes.'

'Thank you,' said the professor. 'If you write her a prescription, please have it charged to me, and also send me your bill.'

'I will,' said the doctor and hung up.

Rosa came into the apartment. 'The doctor told you?' the professor said. 'You aren't pregnant.'

'It's the Virgin's blessing,' said Rosa.

'Indeed, you are lucky.' Speaking quietly, he then told her she would have to go. 'I'm sorry, Rosa, but I simply cannot be constantly caught up in this sort of thing. It upsets me and I can't work.'

'I know.' She turned her head away.

The door bell rang. It was Armando, a small thin man in a long grey overcoat. He was wearing a rakish black Borsalino and a slight moustache. He had dark, worried eyes. He tipped his hat to them.

Rosa told him she was leaving the apartment.

'Then let me help you get your things,' Armando said.

He followed her to the maid's room and they wrapped Rosa's things in newspaper.

When they came out of the room, Armando carrying a shopping bag, Rosa holding a shoe box wrapped in a newspaper, the professor handed Rosa the remainder of her month's wages.

'I'm sorry,' he said again, 'but I have my wife and daughter to think of. They'll be here in a few days.'

She answered nothing. Armando, smoking a cigarette butt, gently opened the door for her and they left together.

Later the professor inspected the maid's room and saw that Rosa had taken all her belongings but the shoes he had given her. When his wife arrived in the apartment, shortly before Thanksgiving, she gave the shoes to the portinaia, who wore them a week, then gave them to her daughter-in-law.

Suppose A Wedding
[A SCENE OF A PLAY]

MAURICE FEUER *is a retired Jewish actor trying to influence his daughter* ADELE *in her choice of a husband. She is engaged to* LEON SINGER, *a young sporting goods store owner from Newark.* FEUER *approves of* BEN GLICKMAN, *a poor beginning writer in the building – a tenement house off Second Avenue in Manhattan – who seems to share his values in life. At any rate* FEUER *likes him.* FLORENCE FEUER' *the actor's wife, once an actress now a beautician, who has also been around and garnered her kind of wisdom, is all for* LEON. *On a hot mid-August day* LEON *has driven in from New Jersey to surprise* ADELE, *when she arrives home from work, and take her to dinner. As the curtain rises,* LEON, *while waiting for her, is playing cards with the actor. Because of the heat the apartment door is open and people occasionally pass by in the hall.*

LEON [*quietly*] : Rummy. This one is mine. [*He puts down his cards and begins to add up the score.*]
FEUER [*rising and pushing back his chair, the* ACTOR *removes his glasses, and without warning, declaims emotionally in Yiddish*] : My God, you're killing your poor father, this is what you're doing. For your whole life I worked bitter hard to take care of you the way a father should. To feed and clothe you. To give you the best kind of education. To teach you what's right. And so how do you pay me back? You pay me back by becoming a tramp. By living with a married man, a cheap, dirty person who has absolutely no respect for you. A bum who used you like

dirt. Worse than dirt. And now when he doesn't want you any more and kicks you out of his bed, you come to me crying, begging I should take you back. My daughter, for what I went through with you, there's no more forgiveness. My heart is milked of tears. It's like a piece of rock. I don't want to see you again in my whole life. Go, but remember, you killed your father. [*He hangs his head.*]

LEON [*perplexed*]: What's that about?

FEUER [*assuming his identity as he puts on his glasses*]: Don't you understand Yiddish?

LEON: Only some of the words.

FEUER: Tst-tst [*sitting*]. It's from a play I once played in the Second Avenue Theatre, 'Sein Tochter's Geliebter'. I was brilliant in this part – magnificent. All the critics raved about me even though the play was schmaltz. Even the *New York Times* sent somebody and he wrote in his review that Maurice Feuer is not only a wonderful actor, he is also a magician. What I could do with such a lousy play was unbelievable. I made it come to life. I made it believable.

[LEON *begins to deal out a new hand as* FEUER *goes on*]

FEUER: I also played in 'Greener Felder', 'Ghosts', 'The Dybbuk', 'The Cherry Orchard', 'Nachds fon Kinder', 'Gott fon Nachoma', and 'Yoshe Kalb'. Schwartz played Reb Melech and I played Yoshe. I was brilliant – marvellous. The play ran three years in New York, and after we played in London, Paris, Prague and Warsaw. We also brought it for a season in South America and played it in Rio, then for sixteen weeks in Buenos Aires....

[*Struck by a memory* FEUER *falls silent.*]

LEON: It's your move.

[*The* ACTOR *absently takes a card and without looking gets rid of another.* LEON *picks up a card, examines it carefully, then drops it among the discards.*]

LEON: Your move.

FEUER: This piece I recited to you is a father talking to his daughter. She took the wrong man and it ruined her life.

[LEON, *examining his cards, has nothing to say.*]

FEUER [*needling a little*] : You couldn't understand it?

LEON: Only partly. Still in all, when I had to I was able to give directions in Yiddish to an old baba with a wig who I met in downtown Newark, on how to get to Brooklyn, New York.

[*As they talk they continue the rummy game.*]

FEUER: Adele knows Yiddish perfect. She learned when she was a little girl. She used to write me letters in Yiddish – they were brilliant. She also had a wonderful handwriting.

LEON: Maybe she'll teach our kids.

[*He is unaware of* FEUER *regarding him ironically.*]

FEUER [*trying a new tack*] : Do you know something about Jewish history?

LEON [*amiably*] : Not very much. [*Afterthought.*] If you're worried about religion, don't worry. I was Bar Mitzvahed.

FEUER: I'm not worried about anything. Tell me, do you know any of the big Yiddish writers – Peretz, Sholem Aleichem, Asch?

LEON: I've heard about them.

FEUER: Do you read serious books?

LEON: Sure, I belong to the Book Find Club.

FEUER: Why don't you pick your own books? Why did you go to college for?

LEON: I mostly do. It's no harm to belong to a good book club, it saves you time. [*Looking at his wrist watch.*] What time is Adele due? It's getting late.

FEUER: Why didn't you telephone her so she would know you were coming? It's not expensive to telephone.

LEON: I thought I'd give her a surprise. My brother Mortie

came into Newark this morning, and he did me the favour to take over the shop so I could get away early. We keep open Wednesday nights.

FEUER [*consulting an old pocket watch*] : She's late.

LEON: Rummy. I win again. [*He shows his cards.*]

FEUER [*hiding his annoyance*] : But my best roles were in Shakespeare – 'Shylock, der Yid,' 'Hamlet, der Yeshiva Bucher' – I was wonderful in the kaddish scene for his father, the dead king. And I also played 'Kaynig Lear und sein Tochter'.

[*Rising and again removing his glasses, he recites in English*] :

'Down from the waist they are centaurs,
Though women all above;
But to the girdle do the gods inherit,
Beneath is all the fiends':
There's hell, there's darkness, there's the
Sulphurous pit,
Burning, scalding, stench, consumption. Fie, fie,
Fie, poh, poh. Give me an ounce of civet good
Apothecary, to sweeten my imagination.'

[LEON, *as though this were not news to him, finishes adding up the score. He shuffles the cards thoroughly as* FEUER *puts on his glasses, and sitting, regards him objectively.*]

LEON: Another game? We're running even now, two and two. Almost the same points.

FEUER: The last one.

        [LEON *deals again and the game goes on.*]

FEUER [*after playing a card, continuing to needle*] : Tell me, Leon, do you like tragedy?

LEON: Do I like it?

FEUER: Do you like to see a tragedy on the stage or read tragic books?

LEON: I can take it or leave it. Generally my nature is cheerful.

FEUER [*building*]: But you went to college. You're a good business man. Adele says you read the *New York Times* every day. In other words you're an intelligent person. So answer me this question: Why do all the best writers and poets write tragedy? And why does every theatre play such plays and all kinds of people pay their good money to see tragedies? Why is that?

LEON: To tell the truth, I never had occasion to give it much thought.

FEUER [*a touch of malice*]: Do me a favour, think about it now.

LEON [*wary*]: I'm not so sure I can tell you exactly but I suppose it's because a lot of life is like that. You realize what's what.

FEUER: What do you mean, 'suppose'? Don't you know for sure? Think what we live through every day – accidents, murders, sickness, disappointments. The thought of death alone is enough.

LEON [*subdued*]: I know what you mean.

FEUER [*sarcasm evident*]: You think you know. Do you really know the condition of human existence? Do you know what the universe means? I'm not talking about who's dead but also about millions of people – in the millions – who live for nothing. They have nothing but poverty, disease, suffering. Or they live in a prison like the Russians. Is this your idea of a good life for everybody?

[BEN GLICKMAN *appears at the doorway, looks in hungrily, sees* LEON *and goes on his way upstairs. Neither of the card players has noticed him.*]

LEON: I wouldn't say that.

FEUER: If you know, you know conditions and you got to do something about them. A man has to be interested to ask for change where it is necessary, to help which way he can.

LEON: I try to help. I give regularly to charity, including the United Jewish Appeal.

FEUER: This isn't enough.

LEON: What do you do?

FEUER [*laying down his cards; emotionally*] : What do I do? I suffer for those who suffer. My heart bleeds for all the injustice in this world.

[LEON *is silently studying his cards.*]

FEUER [*picking up his hand, speaking quietly though still with a purpose*] : Do you ever think what happens to you – inside your soul, when you see a tragic play, for instance Shakespeare?

LEON [*suddenly recalling*] : I feel a catharsis through pity and terror.

FEUER [*after a pause*] : Don't quote me your college books. A writer writes tragedy so people don't forget that they are human. He shows us the conditions that exist. He organizes for us the meaning of our lives so it is clear to our eyes. That's why he writes it, that's why we play it. My best roles were tragic roles. I enjoyed them the most though I was also marvellous in comedy. 'Leid macht auch lachen.'

[*He laughs dramatically, then quietly draws a card and lays down his hand triumphantly.*] Rummy!

LEON: You win. [*He begins to tote up the score.*] I guess I owe you exactly fifty-one cents. [*Taking out his change purse he puts down two quarters and a penny and gently pushes the money towards* FEUER's *side of the table.*]

FEUER [*casually; ignoring the money*] : So how is the baseball situation now, Leon?

SUPPOSE A WEDDING

LEON [*He bites*] : I think the Yanks and Dodgers are leading as usual. [*Catching on.*] I'm afraid I'm not following
the situation very closely, Mr Feuer.

FEUER: If you don't follow it, what do you talk about to
your sporting goods customers?

LEON [*patiently*] : Different things, though not necessarily
sports. People are people – they talk about a lot of things.
[*He slides the three coins a bit farther forward.*] You
better put this away, Mr Feuer.

FEUER: I'm not worried about the money. I play because I
like to play. [*A thought strikes him.*] You know the story
about the famous rabbi and the rich man? He was rich
and a miser. The rabbi took him to the window and said,
'What do you see, tell me?' The rich man looked and he
said, 'I see the street, what else should I see?' 'What's in
the street?' 'What's in the street?' said the rich Jew,
'people – they're walking in the street.' Then the rabbi
took him to a mirror in the room and he said, 'What do
you see now?' 'What do I see now?' said the rich man.
'Naturally I see myself, of course.' 'Aha,' said the rabbi.
'You'll notice in the window is glass, and there is also
glass in the mirror. But the glass in the mirror has silver
painted on the back, and once there's the silver you stop
seeing everybody else and you only see yourself.'

LEON [*still patient*] : The way I look at it is this. Rummy is
a game of chance. If you play for cash the loser pays with
cash and the winner accepts with good grace.

[*Again he slides the coins towards* FEUER.]

FEUER [*pushing them back*] : Please don't tell me about
manners. About manners I knew before you were born.

LEON: Mr Feuer, if you want to insult me, there are better
ways.

FEUER: Why should I insult you?

LEON: Please don't think I am a dope. It's as plain as anyone's nose that you don't like me though I wish I knew why.

FEUER: I'll tell you why if you'll kindly tell me what you are living for ? What is your philosophy of life ?

LEON: I live because I'm alive.

FEUER: Good, but what do you *want* from your life ? That's also important.

LEON [*beginning to show irritation*] : That's my business. Listen, Mr Feuer, don't think I am so dense that I don't understand the reasons for this inquisition you gave me. You pretend you are cordial but it's for the purpose of needling me. I'm not so dense that I don't know what you're insinuating – that I'm not interested in the right things and also that I'm money conscious. But that's all a camouflage. You have some pretty strong prejudices and that's why you're annoyed that Adele is going to marry me.

FEUER: That's a father's pivilege.

LEON: I guess you have no respect for your daughter's judgement.

FEUER: I have plenty of respect but she isn't your type. I don't say you're a bad person but you aren't the right man for her.

LEON: Who's the right man ?

FEUER: More an artistic type. Like her own nature.

LEON: That's just what I figured you would say, and if you'll excuse me, it's a batty point of view. A man is a man, not a profession. I've worked darn hard all my life for everything I have. I got myself a decent education which I paid for myself, even if it isn't a B.A. education. No matter what you think, if you look around, the world doesn't run on art. What it runs on I'm not going to argue with you but I'll say this. At the least you ought to respect me if for no other reason, then because your daughter does. Just because I'm no longhair writer doesn't make me unworthy of her, or for that matter it doesn't make Adele unworthy of me. [*Rising.*] Someday I hope you'll wake up to the facts of life.

[FLORENCE FEUER *appears on the stairs and momentarily pauses when she hears voices.*]

LEON: People aren't the same as their businesses. I am not what I sell. And even if I happened to sell irradiated toilet seats, I still wouldn't worship them. I would use them for the purpose that they are intended.

[FLORENCE *enters the apartment.*]

FEUER: Whatever you sell or don't sell, if Adele marries somebody she don't love, she'll regret it.

FLORENCE [*gasping*]: Feuer – for God's sake! Leon, don't believe him –

LEON [*to* FLORENCE]: Hello, Mrs Feuer. When Adele comes home, tell her I'll be back to take her out to dinner. [*He leaves with dignity.*]

[FLORENCE *sits down in the chair* LEON *has just occupied and slowly removes her shoes. For a minute she sits there not saying a word. The* ACTOR *is silent, too, then goes to the sink and pours himself a long glass of water. He stands there drinking thirstily.*]

FLORENCE [*with weary bitterness*]: What's the matter, Feuer, aren't you satisfied with all your miseries? What do you want from this poor girl's life? Do you hate her?

FEUER [*coolly*]: I'm doing her a favour.

FLORENCE: To ruin her life?

FEUER: To save it. This boy means well but he's a first-class mediocrity. I'm convinced for sure now.

FLORENCE [*wearily patient*]: Are you blind? Take your eyes in your hand and look again. How can you stay in the same room with Leon and not see what a fine person he is? The trouble is you're jealous.

FEUER: If I wasn't jealous of Maurice Schwartz why should I be jealous of Leon Singer?

FLORENCE: Why did you insult him for nothing?

FEUER: Who insulted him?

FLORENCE: You did. Why did he leave with his face so red?

FEUER: What am I, a diagnostician? All I asked him was a few honest questions. It's a father's privilege.

FLORENCE: I can imagine what you asked him.

FEUER: I asked him what he lived for. I asked him what's his philosophy, if any. I have a right to know.

FLORENCE: Why don't you ask yourself and leave him alone?

FEUER: I didn't ask him anything I don't ask myself.

FLORENCE: Please leave him alone. Adele picked him, not you. She's marrying him, not you. Leave them alone before you start a calamity.

FEUER: My opinion is she don't love him.

FLORENCE: Are you crazy? Who told you such a thing?

FEUER: She's not in love, she thinks she is.

FLORENCE: What are you now, a fortune teller? – Miss Lonelyhearts? Have you loved so well that you know all about it?

FEUER: How well I loved *I* know. I also know her and I know she doesn't really love him.

FLORENCE: And I know you encouraged this boy upstairs to come here on his night off. Don't think I don't know you asked her to go out with him.

FEUER: She didn't go because he didn't ask. But yesterday he called her to go for a walk tonight, and she said yes.

FLORENCE [*rising*]: Oh my God. [*She cracks her knuckles on her breasts.*] Does Leon know?

FEUER: Who cares if he knows?

FLORENCE [*angrily*]: Feuer, if you break up this engagement I will leave you. Cook your own vegetables.

[FEUER *glares at her.*]

FLORENCE: You ought to be ashamed to do this to her. What can she get from a poor writer without a steady job – even without a college education that you talk so much about – who writes all day without success?

FEUER: First you learn your art, then you have success. Some day he'll be a first-class writer.

FLORENCE: How do you know?

FEUER: He read me a story – it was brilliant.

FLORENCE: One story don't mean a thing.

FEUER: One is all I need.

FLORENCE [*intensely*]: What can a starving writer give her? A decent home? Can he afford to have children? Will he consider her first when she needs him, or his egotism? I want her to have a future, not a cold-water flat with a poor man.

FEUER: Maybe he won't be rich but he'll have a rich life. With him she could have a real excitement in her life – not a middle-class existence where the real pleasure is to go shopping for something you don't need. Don't underestimate Ben Glickman. I talked to him many times and I know his nature. This is a passionate man – how many are left in the world? He doesn't tell me what he has suffered but I can see in his eyes. He knows what life means and he knows what's real. He'll be good for Adele. He will understand her and love her like she needs to be loved.

FLORENCE: To me he looks sick, like a starved animal. And what are you talking about love when she doesn't even know him? What kind of foolishness is this? It's because you see yourself in him, that's who you see. You see another egoist.

FEUER: Who can talk to you? You're full of foolish anxieties you want to give me.

FLORENCE: Who else can I give them to?

FEUER: This isn't talk, it's confusion.

FLORENCE: You confuse her. Soon she won't know what she's doing. You confused me too.

FEUER: You confused yourself.

FLORENCE [*angrily*]: Egoist! Egoist! You don't deserve to have such a son-in-law.

FEUER [*sarcastic*]: Did I deserve to have such a wife?

FLORENCE [*rising*]: Never, you never deserved me.

[*She picks up her shoes, drops them into the living-room closet, and steps into slippers. Returning to the kitchen she opens the refrigerator door, takes out a few things, and begins wordlessly to prepare supper.* FEUER *is thumbing through a magazine she had brought home. After a minute* FLORENCE *goes to the hall door and quietly shuts it.*]

FEUER [*without turning his head*]: Don't close the door, it's too hot.

FLORENCE [*quietly*]: I want to talk to you one minute – private.

FEUER: Talk. But keep the door open. I'm suffocating.

FLORENCE: Please, Feuer, stop exaggerating. Stop performing. You won't die. All I want to do is talk to you without the neighbours' ears in our door.

FEUER [*shouting*]: Leave the door open I told you.

FLORENCE [*opening it*]: You make me sick!

FEUER [*rising to the occasion*]: You made me sick!

FLORENCE [*though not wanting to, losing her temper*]: Blame yourself. You were sick to begin with from the day I met you. You spoiled my life.

FEUER: You spoiled it yourself.

FLORENCE [*vehemently*]: No, you spoiled it. You don't know where to stop. Every time you stab yourself you stab

me twice. I used to be a nice person but you spoiled my
nature. You're impossible to live with and impossible to
talk to. You don't even converse any more. When you
open your mouth, right away you're yelling – it's always
an argument.

FEUER: Who else is yelling if I may ask you?

FLORENCE: You spoiled my character.

FEUER: I didn't interfere with existing conditions.

FLORENCE [*on the verge of tears*]: You did, you did!

FEUER: If you believe this, you're lying to yourself.

FLORENCE: You're the one who lied. You lied about the
choristers you couldn't stay away from, even with a wife
and child. I gave you my love but you couldn't say no to
the chorus girls. If one of them looked at you you turned
into a rooster. You had no will.

FEUER: I have a *magnificent* will.

FLORENCE: If her garter was loose you took off her stock-
ing. If she took it off herself you helped her to take off the
other.

FEUER [*bitterly*]: And which two-bit actors took off your
stockings? And how many times in your married life?

FLORENCE: You started the whole dirty business. *You*
started it. I never wanted that kind of a life, it wasn't my
nature.

FEUER: It went on for years.

FLORENCE: You left me three times, once two whole years.
Also many times you were on the road for months when I
couldn't go. I was human. I made mistakes.

FEUER: You could've thought of your child instead of sending her from one place to another, in the hands of strangers who made her sick.

FLORENCE: Feuer, for God's sake, I can't stand any more.
Why didn't you take care of her? Because you weren't
there. Because you were busy in bed with somebody else.

FEUER [*blazing*] : You son of a bitch!

[FLORENCE *stares at him, then seems to crumple and slowly lowers herself into a chair. She puts her hands on the table, palms up, and lowering her head, sobs into them. She sobs with her whole body, a wailing weeping.*]

[FEUER *goes to the door and quietly shuts it. He attempts to approach her but can't. He goes to the sink for another glass of water but pours it out without drinking, staring vaguely out the window. Wandering to the mirror, he stands there looking at himself, not enjoying what he sees. Gradually* FLORENCE *stops crying, raises her head and sits quietly at the table, one hand shading her eyes. After a while she blows her nose, and wipes her eyes with a handkerchief.* FEUER, *after glaring at his image, in weariness lies down on the day bed.*]

FLORENCE [*very quietly*] : What's that smell?

FEUER [*wearily*] : Gas.

FLORENCE : What kind of gas?

FEUER : Human gas. Whatever you smell you want immediate identification.

FLORENCE [*after a while*] : Don't you feel well?

FEUER : Perfect.

FLORENCE [*still quietly*] : Did you take your pills today?

FEUER : I took. [*He jumps up from the bed and speaks suddenly, vehemently.*] Florence, I'm sorry. In my heart I love you. My tongue is filthy but not my heart.

FLORENCE [*after a pause*] : How can you love a son of a bitch?

FEUER : Don't poison me with my words. I have enough poison in me already. I say what I don't mean.

FLORENCE : What do you mean?

FEUER : I say that too.

FLORENCE [*still half stunned*] : How can anyone love a son of a bitch?

167

FEUER [*savagely striking his chest*] : I am the son of a bitch.

FLORENCE [*musing*] : It's my fault. I shouldn't fight with you. I don't know why I do it. Maybe it's change of life. What am I changing? Where is my life? It's true, I neglected her, she's the one who suffered. I still feel terrible about those days. But you left me. I had to work. I was out all day. At night I was afraid to be alone. I began to look for company. I was ashamed to let her see me so I sent her away. There was nobody to send her to so I sent her to strangers.

FEUER [*unable to restrain it*] : To friends of your lovers. To their relatives too.

FLORENCE : Have mercy on me, Feuer. My lovers I buried long ago. They're all dead. Don't dig them out of their graves. For what I did to my child I still suffer. You don't have to hurt me more. I know how to hurt myself. [*She cries quietly.*]

[*The* ACTOR *approaches her chair and stands behind her.*]

FEUER : I was a fool. I didn't know what I was doing. I didn't understand my own nature. I talked big but accomplished nothing. Even as an actor I wasn't one of the best. Thomashefsky, Jacob Adler, Schwartz – all were better than me. Their names are famous. Two years off the stage and my name is dead. This is what I deserve – I don't fool myself.

FLORENCE : You were a good actor.

FEUER : I wasn't a good actor and I am not a good man.

[*She rises and they embrace.*]

FLORENCE : I forgave you but you don't forgive me.

FEUER : I don't forgive myself.

FLORENCE [*again remembering*] : Three times you left me.

FEUER : I always came back.

FLORENCE : It took so long. I hurt her so much. [*She wipes her eyes with her fingers.*]

FEUER: Enough now. It was my fault too. I hurt her and I hurt you. Why did I hurt you? – because you were there to hurt. You were the only one [*he pauses – there was another but he doesn't say so*] – the only one who could stand me.

FLORENCE: You try to be good.

FEUER: No.

FLORENCE: Yes. [*After a minute.*] Please do me a favour, Feuer, and I won't ask for anything else – let Leon alone. Let Adele alone. Let them find their life together. It's all I ask you. For her sake – or there will be terrible trouble. [*The door opens and* ADELE *enters, discovering them in each other's arms.*]

ADELE [*sadly*] : Ah, you've been fighting again. [*She shuts the door.*]

[FLORENCE *goes to the sink, washes her eyes with cold water and then dries them with a kitchen towel.* FEUER, *after kissing* ADELE, *goes to the bathroom.*]

ADELE [*putting her purse and a paper down on the table*] : What were you fighting about?

FLORENCE: We weren't fighting. It was a disagreement. Leon was here.

ADELE: Leon? When?

FLORENCE: He came to surprise you. He wants you to eat dinner with him. Please, darling, go. He'll be right back in a few minutes.

ADELE: Where is he now?

FLORENCE: I don't know. I wasn't here. Papa told me. I think they were playing rummy and he said something to Leon.

ADELE: Nasty?

FLORENCE: Papa got sarcastic and Leon didn't like it. But he said he would come back soon.

ADELE: I wasn't expecting him tonight.

FLORENCE: It was a surprise.

ADELE: I wish he had at least called me. I already promised Ben I would go for a walk with him tonight.

FLORENCE: A walk is nothing.

ADELE: I promised.

FLORENCE: Adele, you're an engaged girl. Leon came all the way from Newark to take you to dinner. You ought to go.

ADELE: Being engaged doesn't mean I'm not entitled to a free minute to myself.

FLORENCE: Who said that? All I said was Leon was here. You can tell this boy upstairs you'll see him some other time.

ADELE: He called me up and I said yes.

FLORENCE: It isn't such a big promise.

ADELE: I can't understand why Leon didn't call.

FLORENCE: Call or not call, it's not nice to say no when he's already here. Adele, mamale, please see him tonight. I don't want you to walk with that boy. It's dangerous.

[*She hadn't meant to say quite that.*]

ADELE: A walk isn't a wedding, Mama.

FLORENCE: It could be worse than a wedding.

ADELE: For God's sake, what do you mean?

FLORENCE [*cracking her knuckles on her bosom*]: You can walk to your grave with a little walk.

[FEUER *comes out of the bathroom, looks at himself earnestly in the mirror, mutters something derogatory and enters the kitchen.*]

ADELE: Doesn't anyone trust me?

FEUER: I trust you.

FLORENCE [*to* ADELE]: Is this what you want all your life? [*indicating the apartment.*]

ADELE: I don't see the relationship.

FLORENCE [*deeply troubled*]: For my sake don't go out

170

with this writer. Don't make any more complications in your life. Life is complicated enough.

[*There is a knock on the door.*]

FLORENCE: Come in.

[LEON *enters, carrying a bouquet of flowers.*]

FLORENCE: Leon!

LEON: Hello, everybody. [*To* ADELE]. This is for you, honey.

ADELE: Hello, darling.

[*He hands her the flowers and they kiss.*]

LEON: Hello, Mrs Feuer. Good evening, Mr Feuer.

[*He bears no grudges.*]

FEUER: Good evening.

[ADELE *hands the bouquet to her mother, who hunts for something to put them into. While she is doing that,* FEUER *takes up his newspaper, excuses himself, and after drawing the curtain separating the rooms, sits on the day bed, reading.* FLORENCE, *disapproving the drawn curtain but glad to have* FEUER *out of the way, attends first to the flowers, then fixes her cold supper.* LEON *has seated himself at the table, and* ADELE, *after setting the vase of new flowers on the window sill, is sitting near him.*]

FLORENCE: Leon, would you like to eat with us? It's not much – just a salad with smoked white-fish. Also a few potato pancakes, though not for Feuer – he can't eat them.

LEON: Thanks very much but I was thinking of asking Adele to go out and eat Chinese tonight.

[*He looks at her.*]

ADELE: I'm sorry Leon, if I had known you were coming I would have said yes. That is if you had called before Ben asked me. He's that friend of Papa's who writes. You met him.

LEON [*disappointed*]: Couldn't you break it with him, honey?

ADELE [*hesitantly*] : I'd rather not.

LEON : What's so special about this guy? I mean that you gave him the date? Is it because he's a writer?

ADELE [*defensively*] : You said I could go out once in a while if I felt like it.

LEON : I said it and I stick by it. All I want to know is why you're going out with him?

ADELE : I guess I have the feeling he's gone through a lot.

FLORENCE : Everybody goes through a lot –

ADELE : I like him, he's interesting. I like to talk to him.

LEON : I appreciate his problems but the fact of it is I've come all the way from Newark, New Jersey, to be with the girl I'm engaged to –

FLORENCE : Mamale –

ADELE : Please, Mama –

FLORENCE *removes her apron and retires behind the curtain.* FEUER, *who has been listening, raises his paper as she enters and pretends he's reading.* FLORENCE, *not sure she has made the right move, lights a cigarette and sits in the armchair, flipping through the pages of a magazine.*]

LEON [*lowering his voice*] : Honey, I don't dig it. I thought you'd be surely happy to have this kind of a surprise from me.

ADELE [*gently*] : I am. It's a nice surprise. But all I'm saying is I feel committed tonight. [*Aware of his concern.*] Don't worry, it's not serious. Don't make anything serious out of it. It's just that he's a lonely person, I guess. You feel that when you're with him.

LEON : I'm lonely too. Couldn't you postpone it till tomorrow night?

ADELE : He's off tonight. Tomorrow he works.

LEON : Then till the next time he's off. I'll exchange him tonight for then. [*Again lowering his voice.*] You haven't forgotten our plan to spend a week in the country together in September?

ADELE [*a little cold*] : I don't see what the relationship of this is with that.

LEON : Well, maybe there isn't but why don't you think it over? I mean about tonight.

ADELE : I feel I ought to keep my word with him.

LEON [*edgy*] : What's the matter, Adele – you don't seem cordial at all. What is it, the atmosphere here?

ADELE : If you don't like the atmosphere, why do you come here?

LEON : I don't want to fight with you.

ADELE : I don't want to fight with you.

LEON [*after a minute*] : Maybe you're right. Give me a kiss and I'll call it quits.

ADELE : I'll kiss you because I like you.

[*They kiss.*]

ADELE [*gently*] : I'll postpone it with him if you really want me to.

FEUER [*from behind the curtain*] : Do what *you* want.

FLORENCE [*hushed whisper*] : Please, for God's sake, Feuer.

LEON [*as though he had heard nothing*] : Let's make a compromise. What time is he showing up here?

ADELE : I don't know, around eight, I suppose. He didn't say exactly.

LEON : All right, whatever time. [*He looks at his wristwatch.*] It's ten to six. We can still go out, have our Chinese meal and I'll have you back in the car at fifteen after eight. Then you can go for a short walk and when you come back I'll be waiting and we can drive down to Coney Island.

ADELE : For the first suggestion, okay. I'll go to the Chinese restaurant with you. But I don't want to rush him, while we're walking, to get back for the drive. It's not that kind of date.

LEON [*annoyed*] : What kind of date is it ?

ADELE : A very innocent one.

[*There's a knock on the door.* ADELE *gets up and opens it. Both* FLORENCE *and* FEUER *are attentive.* BEN *enters with a small bouquet of daffodils.*]

BEN : Am I too early ?

[*No one answers as the curtain goes down.*]

The German Refugee

Oskar Gassner sits in his cotton-mesh undershirt and summer bathrobe at the window of his stuffy, hot, dark hotel room on West Tenth Street while I cautiously knock. Outside, across the sky, a late-June green twilight fades in darkness. The refugee fumbles for the light and stares at me, hiding despair but not pain.

I was in those days a poor student and would brashly attempt to teach anybody anything for a buck an hour, although I have since learned better. Mostly I gave English lessons to recently-arrived refugees. The college sent me, I had acquired a little experience. Already a few of my students were trying their broken English, theirs and mine, in the American market place. I was then just twenty, on my way into my senior year in college, a skinny, life-hungry kid, eating himself waiting for the next world war to start. It was a goddamn cheat. Here I was palpitating to get going, and across the ocean Adolph Hitler, in black boots and a square moustache, was tearing up and spitting out all the flowers. Will I ever forget what went on with Danzig that summer?

Times were still hard from the Depression but anyway I made a little living from the poor refugees. They were all over uptown Broadway in 1939. I had four I tutored – Karl Otto Alp, the former film star; Wolfgang Novak, once a brilliant economist; Friedrich Wilhelm Wolff, who had taught medieval history at Heidelberg; and after the night I met him in his disordered cheap hotel room, Oskar Gassner, the Berlin critic and journalist, at one time on the *Acht Uhr*

Abendblatt. They were accomplished men. I had my nerve associating with them, but that's what a world crisis does for people, they get educated.

Oskar was maybe fifty, his thick hair turning grey. He had a big face and heavy hands. His shoulders sagged. His eyes, too, were heavy, a clouded blue; and as he stared at me after I had identified myself, doubt spread in them like underwater currents. It was as if, on seeing me, he had again been defeated. I had to wait until he came to. I stayed at the door in silence. In such cases I would rather be elsewhere but I had to make a living. Finally he opened the door and I entered. Rather, he released it and I was in. 'Bitte,' he offered me a seat and didn't know where to sit himself. He would attempt to say something and then stop, as though it could not possibly be said. The room was cluttered with clothing, boxes of books he had managed to get out of Germany, and some paintings. Oskar sat on a box and attempted to fan himself with his heavy hand. 'Zis heat,' he muttered, forcing his mind to the deed. 'Impozzible. I do not know such heat.' It was bad enough for me but terrible for him. He had difficulty breathing. He tried to speak, lifted a hand, and let it drop like a dead duck. He breathed as though he were fighting a battle; and maybe he won because after ten minutes we sat and slowly talked.

Like most educated Germans Oskar had at one time studied English. Although he was certain he couldn't say a word he managed to put together a fairly decent, if sometimes comical, English sentence. He misplaced consonants, mixed up nouns and verbs, and mangled idioms, yet we were able to communicate. We conversed in English, with an occasional assist by me in pidgin-German or Yiddish, what he called 'Jiddish'. He had been to America before, last year for a short visit. He had come a month before Kristallnacht, when the Nazis shattered the Jewish store windows and burnt all the synagogues, to see if he could find a job for himself; he had no relatives in America and getting a job would permit him quickly to enter the country. He had been promised something, not in journalism, but with the help of a foundation, as a lecturer. Then he returned to Berlin, and after a frightening delay of six months was permitted to emigrate. He had sold whatever he could, managed to get some paintings, gifts of Bauhaus friends, and some boxes of books out by bribing two Dutch border guards; he had said good-bye to his wife and left the accursed country. He gazed at me with cloudy eyes. 'We parted amicably,' he said in German, 'my wife was gentile. Her mother was an appalling anti-Semite. They returned to live in Stettin.' I asked no questions. Gentile is gentile, Germany is Germany.

His new job was in the Institute for Public Studies, in New York. He was to give a lecture a week in the fall term, and during next spring, a course, in English translation, in 'The Literature of the Weimar Republic'. He had never taught before and was afraid to. He was in that way to be introduced to the public, but the thought of giving the lecture in English just about paralysed him. He didn't see how he could do it. 'How is it pozzible? I cannot say two words. I cannot pronounziate. I will make a fool of myself.' His melancholy deepened. Already in the two months since his arrival, and a round of diminishingly expensive hotel rooms, he had had two English tutors, and I was the third. The others had given him up, he said, because his progress was so poor, and he thought he also depressed them. He asked me whether I felt I could do something for him, or should he go to a speech specialist, someone, say, who charged five dollars an hour, and beg his assistance? 'You could try him,' I said, 'and then come back to me.' In those days I figured what I knew, I knew. At that he managed a smile. Still, I wanted him to make up his mind or it would be no confidence down the line. He said, after a while, he would stay with me. If he went to the five-dollar professor it might help his tongue but not his stomach. He would have no money left to eat with. The Institute had paid him in advance for the summer but it was only three hundred dollars and all he had.

He looked at me dully. 'Ich weiss nicht wie ich weiter machen soll.'

I figured it was time to move past the first step. Either we did that quickly or it would be like drilling rock for a long time.

'Let's stand at the mirror,' I said.

He rose with a sigh and stood there beside me, I thin, elongated, red-headed, praying for success, his and mine; Oskar, uneasy, fearful, finding it hard to face either of us in the faded round glass above his dresser.

'Please,' I said to him, 'could you say "right"?'

'Ghight,' he gargled.

'No – right. You put your tongue here.' I showed him where as he tensely watched the mirror. I tensely watched him. 'The tip of it curls behind the ridge on top, like this.'

He placed his tongue where I showed him.

'Please,' I said, 'now say "right".'

Oskar's tongue fluttered. 'Right.'

'That's good. Now say "treasure" – that's harder.'

'Tgheasure.'

'The tongue goes up in front, not in the back of the mouth. Look.'

He tried, his brow wet, eyes straining, 'Trreasure.'

'That's it.'

'A miracle,' Oskar murmured.

I said if he had done that he could do the rest.

We went for a bus ride up Fifth Avenue and then walked for a while around Central Park Lake. He had put on his

German hat, with its hatband bow at the back, a broad-lapelled wool suit, a necktie twice as wide as the one I was wearing, and walked with a small-footed waddle. The night wasn't bad, it had got a bit cooler. There were a few large stars in the sky and they made me sad.

'Do you sink I will succezz?'

'Why not?' I asked.

Later he bought me a bottle of beer.

2

To many of these people, articulate as they were, the great loss was the loss of language – that they could not say what was in them to say. You have some subtle thought and it comes out like a piece of broken bottle. They could, of course, manage to communicate but just to communicate was frustrating. As Karl Otto Alp, the ex-film star who became a buyer for Macy's, put it years later, 'I felt like a child, or worse, often like a moron. I am left with myself unexpressed. What I know, indeed, what I am, becomes to me a burden. My tongue hangs useless.' The same with Oskar it figures. There was a terrible sense of useless tongue, and I think the reason for his trouble with his other tutors was that to keep from drowning in things unsaid he wanted to swallow the ocean in a gulp: Today he would learn English and tomorrow wow them with an impeccable Fourth of July speech, followed by a successful lecture at the Institute for Public Studies.

We performed our lessons slowly, step by step, everything in its place. After Oskar moved to a two-room apartment in a house on West 85th Street, near the Drive, we met three times a week at four-thirty, worked an hour and a half, then, since it was too hot to cook, had supper at the 72nd

Street Automat and conversed on my time. The lessons we divided into three parts: diction exercises and reading aloud; then grammar, because Oskar felt the necessity of it, and composition correction; with conversation, as I said, thrown in at supper. So far as I could see, he was coming along. None of these exercises was giving him as much trouble as they apparently had in the past. He seemed to be learning and his mood lightened. There were moments of elation as he heard his accent flying off. For instance when sink became think. He stopped calling himself 'hopelezz', and I became his 'bezt teacher', a little joke I liked.

Neither of us said much about the lecture he had to give early in October, and I kept my fingers crossed. It was somehow to come out of what we were doing daily, I think I felt, but exactly how, I had no idea; and to tell the truth, though I didn't say so to Oskar, the lecture frightened me. That and the ten more to follow during the fall term. Later, when I learned that he had been attempting with the help of the dictionary to write in English and had produced 'a complete disahster', I suggested maybe he ought to stick to German and we could afterwards both try to put it into passable English. I was cheating when I said that because my German is meagre, enough to read simple stuff but certainly not good enough for serious translation; anyway, the idea was to get Oskar into production and worry about translating later. He sweated with it, from enervating morning to exhausted night, but no matter what language he tried, though he had been a professional writer for a generation and knew his subject cold, the lecture refused to move past page one.

It was a sticky, hot July and the heat didn't help at all.

3

I had met Oskar at the end of June and by the seventeenth of July we were no longer doing lessons. They had foundered on the 'impozzible' lecture. He had worked on it each day in frenzy and growing despair. After writing more than a hundred opening pages he furiously flung his pen against the wall, shouting he could no longer write in that filthy tongue. He cursed the German language. He hated the damned country and the damned people. After that what was bad became worse. When he gave up attempting to write the lecture, he stopped making progress in English. He seemed to forget what he already knew. His tongue thickened and the accent returned in all its fruitiness. The little he had to say was in handcuffed and tortured English. The only German I heard him speak was in a whisper to himself. I doubt he knew he was talking it. That ended our formal work together, though I did drop in every day or so to sit with him. For hours he sat motionless in a large green velours armchair, hot enough to broil in, and through tall windows stared at the colourless sky above 85th Street, with a wet depressed eye.

Then once he said to me, 'If I do not this legture prepare, I will take my life.'

'Let's begin, Oskar,' I said. 'You dictate and I'll write. The ideas count, not the spelling.'

He didn't answer so I stopped talking.

He had plunged into an involved melancholy. We sat for hours, often in profound silence. This was alarming to me, though I had already had some experience with such depression. Wolfgang Novak, the economist, though English came more easily to him, was another. His problems arose mainly, I think, from physical illness. And he felt a greater sense of the lost country than Oskar. Sometimes in the early evening I persuaded Oskar to come with me for a short walk on the Drive. The tail end of sunsets over the Palisades seemed to appeal to him. At least he looked. He would put on full regalia – hat, suit coat, tie, no matter how hot or what I suggested – and we went slowly down the stairs, I wondering whether he would ever make it to the bottom. He seemed to me always suspended between two floors.

We walked slowly uptown, stopping to sit on a bench and watch night rise above the Hudson. When we returned to his room, if I sensed he had loosened up a bit, we listened to music on the radio; but if I tried to sneak in a news broadcast, he said to me, 'Please, I can not more stand of world misery.' I shut off the radio. He was right, it was a time of no good news. I squeezed my brain. What could I sell him? Was it good news to be alive? Who could argue the point? Sometimes I read aloud to him – I remember he liked the first part of *Life on the Mississippi*. We still went to the Automat once or twice a week, he perhaps out of habit, because he didn't feel like going anywhere – I to get him out of his room. Oskar ate little, he toyed with a spoon. His dull eyes looked as though they had been squirted with a dark dye.

Once after a momentary cooling rainstorm we sat on newspapers on a wet bench overlooking the river and Oskar at last began to talk. In tormented English he conveyed his intense and everlasting hatred of the Nazis for destroying his career, uprooting his life after half a century, and flinging him like a piece of bleeding meat to the hawks. He cursed them thickly, the German nation, an inhuman, conscienceless, merciless people. 'They are pigs mazquerading as peacogs,' he said. 'I feel certain that my wife, in her heart, was a Jew hater.' It was a terrible bitterness, an eloquence almost without vocabulary. He became silent again. I hoped to hear more about his wife but decided not to ask.

Afterwards in the dark Oskar confessed that he had attempted suicide during his first week in America. He was living, at the end of May, in a small hotel, and had one night filled himself with barbiturates; but his phone had fallen off the table and the hotel operator had sent up the elevator boy who found him unconscious and called the police. He was revived in the hospital.

'I did not mean to do it,' he said, 'it was a mistage.'

'Don't ever think of it again,' I said, 'it's total defeat.'

'I don't,' he said wearily, 'because it is so arduouz to come back to life.'

'Please, for any reason whatever.'

Afterwards when we were walking, he surprised me by saying, 'Maybe we ought to try now the legture onze more.'

We trudged back to the house and he sat at his hot desk, I trying to read as he slowly began to reconstruct the first page of his lecture. He wrote, of course, in German.

4

He got nowhere. We were back to nothing, to sitting in silence in the heat. Sometimes, after a few minutes, I had to take off before his mood overcame mine. One afternoon I came unwillingly up the stairs – there were times I felt momentary surges of irritation with him – and was frightened to find Oskar's door ajar. When I knocked no one answered. As I stood there, chilled down the spine, I realized I was thinking about the possibility of his attempting suicide again. 'Oskar?' I went into the apartment, looked into both rooms and the bathroom, but he wasn't there. I thought he might have drifted out to get something from a store and took the opportunity to look quickly around. There was nothing startling in the medicine chest, no pills but aspirin, no iodine. Thinking, for some reason, of a gun, I searched his desk drawer. In it I found a thin-paper airmail letter from Germany. Even if I had wanted to, I couldn't read the handwriting, but as I held it in my hand I did make out a sentence: 'Ich bin dir siebenundzwanzig Jahre treu gewesen.' There was no gun in the drawer, I shut it and stopped looking. It had occurred to me if you want to kill yourself all you need is a straight pin. When Oskar returned he said he had been sitting in the public library, unable to read.

Now we are once more enacting the changeless scene, curtain rising on two speechless characters in a furnished apartment, I, in a straightback chair, Oskar in the velours armchair that smothered rather than supported him, his flesh grey, the big grey face, unfocused, sagging. I reached over to switch on the radio but he barely looked at me in a way that begged no. I then got up to leave but Oskar, clearing his throat, thickly asked me to stay. I stayed, thinking, was there more to this than I could see into? His problems, God knows, were real enough, but could there be something more than a refugee's displacement, alienation, financial insecurity, being in a strange land without friends or a speakable tongue? My speculation was the old one; not all drown in this ocean, why does he? After a while I shaped the thought and asked him, was there something below the surface, invisible? I was full of this thing from college, and wondered if there mightn't be some unknown quality in his depression that a psychiatrist maybe might help him with, enough to get him started on his lecture.

He meditated on this and after a few minutes haltingly said he had been psychoanalysed in Vienna as a young man.

'Just the jusual drek,' he said, 'fears and fantazies that afterwaards no longer bothered me.'

'They don't now?'

'Not.'

'You've written many articles and lectures before,' I said. 'What I can't understand, though I know how hard the situation is, is why you can never get past page one.'

He half lifted his hand. 'It is a paralyzis of my will. The whole legture is clear in my mind but the minute I write down a single word – or in English or in German – I have a terrible fear I will not be able to write the negst. As though someone has thrown a stone at a window and the whole house – the whole idea, zmashes. This repeats, until I am dezperate.'

He said the fear grew as he worked that he would die before he completed the lecture, or if not that, he would write it so disgracefully he would wish for death. The fear immobilized him.

'I have lozt faith. I do not – not longer possezz my former values of myself. In my life there has been too much illusion.'

I tried to believe what I was saying: 'Have confidence, the feeling will pass.'

'Confidenze I have not. For this and alzo whatever elze I have lozt I thank the Nazis.'

5

It was by then mid-August and things were growing steadily worse wherever one looked. The Poles were mobilizing for war. Oskar hardly moved. I was full of worries though I pretended calm weather.

He sat in his massive armchair with sick eyes, breathing like a wounded animal.

'Who can write aboud Walt Whitman in such terrible times?'

'Why don't you change the subject?'

'It mages no differenze what is the subject. It is all uzeless.'

I came every day, as a friend, neglecting my other students and therefore my livelihood. I had a panicky feeling that if things went on as they were going they would end in Oskar's suicide; and I felt a frenzied desire to prevent that. What's more, I was sometimes afraid I was myself becoming melancholy, a new talent, call it, of taking less pleasure in my little pleasures. And the heat continued, oppressive, relentless. We thought of escape into the country but neither of us had the money. One day I bought Oskar a second-hand fan – wondering why we hadn't thought of that before – and he sat in the breeze for hours each day, until after a week, shortly after the Soviet–Nazi non-aggression pact was signed, the motor gave out. He could not sleep at night and sat at his desk with a wet towel on his head, still attempting to write his lecture. He wrote reams on a treadmill, it came out nothing. When he slept out of exhaustion he had fantastic frightening dreams of the Nazis inflicting tortures on him, sometimes forcing him to look upon the corpses of those they had slain. In one dream he told me about, he had gone back to Germany to visit his wife. She wasn't home and he had been directed to a cemetery. There, though the tombstone read another name, her blood seeped out of the earth above her shallow grave. He groaned aloud at the memory.

Afterwards he told me something about her. They had met as students, lived together, and were married at twenty-three. It wasn't a very happy marriage. She had turned into a sickly woman, physically unable to have children. 'Something was wrong with her interior strugture.'

Though I asked no questions, Oskar said, 'I offered her to come with me here but she refused this.'

'For what reason?'

'She did not think I wished her to come.'

'Did you?' I asked.

'Not,' he said.

He explained he had lived with her for almost twenty-seven years under difficult circumstances. She had been ambivalent about their Jewish friends and his relatives, though outwardly she seemed not a prejudiced person. But her mother was always a violent anti-Semite.

'I have nothing to blame myself,' Oskar said.

He took to his bed. I took to the New York Public Library. I read some of the German poets he was trying to write about, in English translation. Then I read *Leaves of Grass* and wrote down what I thought one or two of them had got from Whitman. One day, towards the end of August, I brought Oskar what I had written. It was in good part guessing but my idea wasn't to write the lecture for him. He lay on his back, motionless, and listened utterly sadly to what I had written. Then he said, no, it wasn't the love of death they had got from Whitman – that ran through German poetry – but it was most of all his feeling for Bruder-mensch, his humanity.

'But this does not grow long on German earth,' he said, 'and is soon deztroyed.'

I said I was sorry I had got it wrong, but he thanked me anyway.

I left, defeated, and as I was going down the stairs, heard the sound of someone sobbing. I will quit this, I thought, it has gotten to be too much for me. I can't drown with him.

I stayed home the next day, tasting a new kind of private

misery too old for somebody my age, but that same night Oskar called me on the phone, blessing me wildly for having read those notes to him. He had got up to write me a letter to say what I had missed, and it ended by his having written half the lecture. He had slept all day and tonight intended to finish it up.

'I thank you,' he said, 'for much, alzo including your faith in me.'

'Thank God,' I said, not telling him I had just about lost it.

6

Oskar completed his lecture – wrote and rewrote it – during the first week in September. The Nazis had invaded Poland, and though we were greatly troubled, there was some sense of release; maybe the brave Poles would beat them. It took another week to translate the lecture, but here we had the assistance of Friedrich Wilhelm Wolff, the historian, a gentle, erudite man, who liked translating and promised his help with future lectures. We then had about two weeks to work on Oskar's delivery. The weather had changed, and so, slowly, had he. He had awakened from defeat, battered, after a wearying battle. He had lost close to twenty pounds. His complexion was still grey; when I looked at his face I expected to see scars, but it had lost its flabby unfocused quality. His blue eyes had returned to life and he walked with quick steps, as though to pick up a few for all the steps he hadn't taken during those long hot days he had lain torpid in his room.

We went back to our former routine, meeting three late afternoons a week for diction, grammar, and the other exercises. I taught him the phonetic alphabet and transcribed long lists of words he was mispronouncing. He worked many hours trying to fit each sound into place, holding half a match-stick between his teeth to keep his jaws apart as he exercised his tongue. All this can be a dreadfully boring business unless you think you have a future. Looking at him I realized what's meant when somebody is called 'another man'.

The lecture, which I now knew by heart, went off well. The director of the Institute had invited a number of prominent people. Oskar was the first refugee they had employed and there was a move to make the public cognizant of what was then a new ingredient in American life. Two reporters had come with a lady photographer. The auditorium of the Institute was crowded. I sat in the last row, promising to put up my hand if he couldn't be heard, but it wasn't necessary. Oskar, in a blue suit, his hair cut, was of course nervous, but you couldn't see it unless you studied him. When he stepped up to the lectern, spread out his manuscript, and spoke his first English sentence in public, my heart hesitated; only he and I, of everybody there, had any idea of the anguish he had been through. His enunciation wasn't at all bad – a few s's for th's, and he once said bag for back, but otherwise he did all right. He read poetry well – in both languages – and though Walt Whitman, in his mouth, sounded a little as though he had come to the shores of Long Island as a German immigrant, still the poetry read as poetry:

'And I know the spirit of God is the brother of my own,
And that all the men ever born are also my brothers, and
    the women my sisters and lovers,
And that the kelson of creation is love . . .'

Oskar read it as though he believed it. Warsaw had fallen but the verses were somehow protective. I sat back conscious of two things : how easy it is to hide the deepest wounds ; and the pride I felt in the job I had done.

7

Two days later I came up the stairs into Oskar's apartment to find a crowd there. The refugee, his face beet-red, lips bluish, a trace of froth in the corners of his mouth, lay on the floor in his limp pyjamas, two firemen on their knees, working over him with an inhalator. The windows were open and the air stank.

A policeman asked me who I was and I couldn't answer. 'No, oh no.'

I said no but it was unchangeably yes. He had taken his life – gas – I hadn't even thought of the stove in the kitchen.

'Why ?' I asked myself. 'Why did he do it ?' Maybe it was the fate of Poland on top of everything else, but the only answer anyone could come up with was Oskar's scribbled note that he wasn't well, and had left Martin Goldberg all his possessions. I am Martin Goldberg.

I was sick for a week, had no desire either to inherit or investigate, but I thought I ought to look through his things before the court impounded them, so I spent a morning sitting in the depths of Oskar's armchair, trying to read his correspondence. I had found in the top drawer a thin packet of letters from his wife and an airmail letter of recent date from his anti-Semitic mother-in-law.

She writes in a tight script it takes me hours to decipher, that her daughter, after Oskar abandons her, against her own mother's fervent pleas and anguish, is converted to Judaism by a vengeful rabbi. One night the Brown Shirts appear, and though the mother wildly waves her bronze crucifix in their faces, they drag Frau Gassner, together with the other Jews, out of the apartment house, and transport them in lorries to a small border town in conquered Poland. There, it is rumoured, she is shot in the head and topples into an open tank ditch, with the naked Jewish men, their wives and children, some Polish soldiers, and a handful of gipsies.